EMIGRANT TRAIL

Also by B.N. Rundell

Rindin' Lonesome

Star Dancer

The Christmas Bear

Buckskin Chronicles

McCain Chronicles

Plainsman Western Series

Rocky Mountain Saint Series

Stonecroft Saga

EMIGRANT TRAIL

MCCAIN CRONICLES
BOOK SIX

B.N. RUNDELL

WOLFPACK
PUBLISHING
— EST 2013 —

Emigrant Trail
Paperback Edition
Copyright © 2023 B.N. Rundell

Wolfpack Publishing
9850 S. Maryland Parkway, Suite A-5 #323
Las Vegas, Nevada 89183

wolfpackpublishing.com

Paperback ISBN 978-1-63977-871-3
eBook ISBN 978-1-63977-872-0
LCCN 2023947620

DEDICATION

This has been an unusual time for me. I had to have emergency brain surgery and was treated at Penrose Hospital in Colorado Springs, Colorado. I found the entire nursing staff to be exceptional, always helpful, encouraging, and in the best of spirits. So, I dedicate this book to all of the front-line workers, from the helicopter pilot that flew the flight for life with me aboard, to the flight nurses, the emergency room staff at St. Thomas More in Canon City, Co and the entire staff, doctors, nurses, and all the others at Penrose Hospital. You're the best! And I thank you for your exceptional care. It is because of all of you that I was able to finish this book. Thank you.

EMIGRANT TRAIL

Chapter 1

WORD

The ground moved underneath them; a low rumble sounded as if it came from deep within the earth. The big stallion shook, looking side to side and down at the ground. He stared at the trembling trees, the leaves shaking as if in a strong wind but there was no wind. Elijah McCain jumped to the ground, a firm grip on the reins of the big stallion and on the lead rope that usually lay over the neck of the packhorse. Both horses nickered, nostrils flaring, ears pricked as they skittishly moved, tenuous steps side to side, both turning to look at the man standing between them who spoke to them, reached for their necks to stroke and settle them, but he too was looking all around, wide-eyed. It stopped as quickly as it started, dust rising from all around as if the earth had cracked to let out a breath, blowing dust all about and lasting only a few seconds until only the leaves on the trees moved slightly, no more than in a light breeze. The big stallion trembled beside him, the dapple-grey pack horse moving close beside the claybank held by the man, neither ready to take another step, trembling, their muscles ripping across their chests and down their sides. Their hooves side stepped, lifted, pranced about, but the man held them firm and continued to speak, low and slow, encouraging and stroking both animals.

Elijah McCain stepped back into the saddle, reached down to stroke the neck of his claybank stallion and spoke softly as he again reassured the trembling horses, low rumbling nickers coming from deep within, "It's alright, boy. Just a little tremblor. Ain't nuthin' to worry about." He reached over to stroke the face of the grey, "Easy boy, easy now."

Eli breathed deep, rolled his shoulders back and twisted around in the saddle to stretch his muscles and to look at the countryside. Thin clouds of dust wafted about, small rocks slid off steep slopes, tumbling to the bottom and leaving debris in its path. He stood tall, looking around the heavily timbered slope, but wherever there was a break in the trees, he could see the distant trees waving as if the tremblor was traveling before him. He shook his head, stroked the horses necks again, and nudged them forward, both man and animals uncertain of each step.

Eli was tired, tired of riding, tired of the search, tired of always being one step behind. He started his search in the early spring of 1867 when his wife, Margaret, lay on her death bed, gripping his hand tightly as she pleaded with him, "Bring my boys home, promise me, bring them home. There's so much here for them to do and to have a good future. They made a terrible mistake, I know, but please forgive them and bring them home." She dropped her eyes, sighed heavily, "If only...if only I could see them one more time…" and turned to look at Eli, her husband of almost twenty years. "You've been so kind, and all because of your loyalty to Ferdy, such a dear friend." She paused, tried to squeeze his hand and coughed, struggling for air, "I loved you. You know that don't you?"

"Yes Margaret, and I have loved you. Sure, we didn't start off like most couples, but…" he shrugged. "I only wish I could have had more time with you."

She forced a smile, "Please Eli, bring them home. Promise me you will, please?" she begged as tears filled her eyes and she squeezed his hand.

"I promise, I'll do whatever I have to, and I'll tell them everything. I promise."

Margaret forced a smile, sighed her last breath and her eyes lost their sparkle, her hands slipped from his, and she lay unmoving.

He remembered those moments as if he was sitting at her bedside now, but it was the hard saddle on the hurricane deck of his long-legged claybank stallion, Rusty, and Grey, the mustang pack horse followed, free rein, keeping within a step of his trail partner. They were headed south, bound for Monterey, California, where the boys, twins, Jubal and Joshua Paine, were thought to be, in pursuit of two girls they met on the Clipper ship, *Flying Cloud*. He knew they had been shanghaied in Astoria, Oregon, but they had a history of quitting things, they had deserted the army before the end of the war and long before their enlistment was finished. They had quit on the captain of the riverboat, choosing to hire on with a freighter company that would take them to the goldfields of Montana. And they had bailed out of their commitment to a freighter to try their hand at gold panning.

Now he had suspected they would jump ship at the first opportunity and according to Captain Creesy of the *Flying Cloud* they had. But this time they were chasing after a pair of young women, sisters, that lived in Monterey.

The young men were his stepsons, born just a few months after he wed their mother, the result of another promise made to his close friend, Ferdinand Paine, a West Point classmate and companion on their first field assignment at Jefferson Barracks, Missouri. Ferdy, as he was known to friends and family, had taken a bullet from a southern sympathizer when a handful of them were confronted by the Union forces and dispersed, but not before a bit of a skirmish. When Ferdy lay dying in his arms, he had pleaded with Eli to take care of his wife, who was expecting their first child. He agreed and married the woman who birthed twins six months after the wedding. Jubal and Joshua had taken the name of their natural father and, with an absentee step-father in the military, had lacked something in their upbringing.

And Elijah McCain had grown tired of the chase, although he suspected the boys thought he was chasing them because they deserted the army and he, a career soldier, was after them to return them to the ranks and pay the penalty of desertion. But he had mustered out of the service, choosing to make his life with his wife and boys, although things don't always work out as expected. He had made a promise, and he was the kind of man that always kept his word, especially to a dying woman, and that covenant had driven him across most of the continent, and hopefully, it would soon end.

He nudged Rusty on, mid-morning was no time to stop and from what he knew of earthquakes, what they had just experienced was probably all that would happen.

The country south of San Francisco, was still wild country. Heavily timbered, rocky ridges, high hills, some called them mountains but once you've seen the Rocky Mountains, he could not think of these as mountains.

An old-timer in the small settlement of Millbrae, just south of San Francisco and on the grounds of Rancho Buri Buri, had given him some guidance as to the roads and trails that would take him to the Monterey area. "It's a good week, mebbe ten days ridin'. O'er a hunnert mile and up an' down, twist aroun', heavy timber, grizzly bears, black bears, panters, wolves, coyotes, bobcats, lynx, and pro'ly some long clawed, big fangs, things they ain't got names fer!" He shook his head, chuckling, "An' that ain't countin' the Injuns an' outlaws an' them Mex bandito gangs, sonny boy, an' I been hearin' 'bout a renegade name o' Glotón, one o' them Costanoan Rumsen Ohlone people the gov'ments been tryin' to get on a res down south, but he ain't happy 'bout it. Been stealin' hosses, kilt a few lone travelers, gold hunters an' the like, they say he's a wild one and sneaky, no tellin' how many white folks he done kilt an' scalped. You'd think he was one o' them plains Injuns, you know, like the Sioux or Blackfeet. Reckon you best be ready fer just 'bout anythin'!" he cackled as he walked off. Even though the old-timer was probably exaggerating beyond measure when it came to the animals and outlaws, Eli trusted him as to the trails he talked about. And it was on one of those trails that Eli traveled now, and it had all the look of an ancient path used by the many native hunters and travelers before the land was settled by the Spanish or the whites. It also had the tracks and sign of the many migrating animals of the wilderness. He traveled southwest from Millbrae, crossed over a long ridge and took to the trail that often straddled the ridge, but rode mostly on the west shoulder of the long ridge.

He saw the claw marks that dug deep into the bark of tall pines, reaching as high as he could reach as he stood in his stirrups, which would mean the bear that made his mark would stand about eight feet tall. Other trees showed sign where deer and elk scraped velvet off their antlers in late summer, lower down porcupine had gnawed at the bark, leaving their musky scent on the trees.

Often he would see stone cairns at junctions in the trail, used by the natives to mark the chosen trail used by their people. With a carpet of pine needles and leaves from redbud, sycamore, boxelder and oak, the horses moved quietly along the trail that was shouldered above the narrow, twisting valley below. As the sun was nearing its zenith, he took a wisp of a trail that branched off to the west, crossed the dry creek bed in the bottom of the long draw, and climbed into the trees of a higher ridge. A bit of a bald shoulder offered deep grass, monkeyflower and sage for a mid-day break and Eli nudged the big stallion to the shade of a cluster of tall ponderosa and nearby buckeye and stepped down.

The chuckle of water from the thicket of trees offered Eli the chance for the coffee he failed to have this morning. He dug out the coffee pot, started a hat-sized fire under the wide branches of the ponderosa and walked to the little spring fed creek and filled the pot, rinsed out his cup and with the cup and pot full, returned to the clearing. Once the pot was on the fire and the flames licked hungrily around it, he led the horses, that were enjoying the green grass in the shade, to the little creek and let them take their water, then returned to the clearing and settled down in the shade, his companion, Lobo, the black wolf-dog that had adopted him and the horses, watching the pot that was beginning its dance.

He absent-mindedly ran his fingers through the scruff of Lobo's collar, thinking about his search for the boys and the many miles already traveled from the horse farm in Kentucky that had been his wife's family's farm. He had ridden to St. Louis, took a riverboat to Fort Benton, Montana territory, covered most of the gold fields of Montana, followed their trail to Fort Walla Walla, Washington and on to the Columbia River all the way to Astoria, Oregon. It was there he discovered the boys had been shanghaied and taken aboard the *Flying Cloud* clipper ship that was bound to the south and beyond. From Astoria, he had taken a riverboat to Portland and ridden south through Oregon and northern California. Only to discover the boys had jumped ship in San Francisco and were bound for Monterey. He shook his head as he thought of his journey and that of the boys, but for whatever reason, maybe it was because the boys were pursuing two women they met on the boat, that he was more hopeful than usual that the end of his search was nearing.

Eli started to reach for the coffee pot, but a low growl from Lobo gave him pause. He glanced down to see where Lobo was looking and looked to the trees just beyond the horses. He casually dropped his right hand across his middle to lay his hand on the butt of his holstered Colt that sat on his left hip, butt forward. He bent forward to reach for the pot with his left hand and spoke in a normal voice, "I've got coffee if you're of a mind. Come on in with your hands clear and I'll share it with you."

Nothing moved, no answer came, but Lobo's nostrils flared, and his head was held erect, and he slowly came to his feet, lowered his head and let another low growl come, his lip curled back to expose his white fangs, his scruff standing tall and his body tense, ready to attack. Eli whispered, "Easy boy, easy."

CHAPTER 2

VISITOR

The shadows in the thicket of trees moved, paused, moved again and stepped into the light as he neared the clearing and the small cookfire of Eli. A tall figure, dark skinned, well-muscled and almost naked stood before him. He spoke, "You travel the way of the ancients."

Eli nodded slowly, "Yes. I have seen sign of the ancients and the many animals of the forests, but little sign of the people of the land."

The man took another tentative step closer, the light from the fire accenting the muscular stature and stoic expression of the man. Eli looked as he slowly stood before the visitor to see a man unlike any other he had seen. Thick black hair was drawn up into a large bun that was wrapped in a wide band of intricately woven discs carved from the shells of abalone, oyster, and mussels. The iridescent colors were arranged to make a subtle design at the forefront of the wide band that spanned the width of a man's outstretched hand. Bordered by darker colored beads that appeared to be carved wood or bone, the headdress stood atop his head, circumventing the large bun of his hair, loose ends standing and groomed to make a border of spiked hair dyed a bluish grey color that masked a tall but smaller bun that stood at the top of the bun to hold the remnant of hair that stood straight up, interspersed with multi colored feathers. A wide band of silver shone at the top of the man's biceps that appeared to accent dark tattoos that covered his upper arm. His right ear was pierced with a small container that reminded Eli of the medicine bundles often carried by the plains tribes. His only clothing resembled a breech cloth, but where the plains tribes had a long cloth that looped over a belt or cord, under the crotch and over the same belt at the back, with the wide ends hanging free and often decorated with beaded designs, this cloth was plain and tucked inside the belt, the only design being dyed colors of irregular shapes or stripes. A long strip of rawhide over his left shoulder held a quiver with a bow and arrows at his right waist and another strip held a possible pouch under his left arm. He held a brass mounted Henry .44 before him, across his chest, unthreatening but held ready to use.

Eli had noticed the hammer on the Henry was not cocked and knew the man would have to jack a round, turn to his off side, before he could fire and in that time he could draw his Colt and fire. He felt safe and confident and said, "I am Eli. You are welcome to share my coffee and my camp," waving the man to the log across the fire from where he stood.

"I am Glotón," he answered and stepping closer, he squatted on his haunches, waiting for Eli to return to his seat on the rock.

Eli nodded, stepped to the packs and retrieved

another cup, sat on the rock and poured a cup of coffee for the man, offering it to him.

Glotón accepted, brought the cup to his lips, took a deep breath of the java and slowly sipped from the cup. He looked up to Eli who was also drinking his coffee and asked, "Why are you here?"

"I am traveling to Monterey." Eli looked around, nodded to the woods from where his visitor came and asked, "Is this your home?"

"All of this land is the home of my people. We are called the Costanoans, but my mother was Yokut. When the black robes came and built their missions, the many people lost who they were and have been destroyed," he growled, hatred blazing in his eyes. "Then whites, like you, came to take the gold from the land and wherever they went, they killed the people! The black robes tried to make us serve their gods and become like them, the gold-hunters just wanted to destroy us all! Most of the people that lived after the soldiers killed so many, have been taken from their homes and their lands and put where no real people can live, and they die!" he spat the words, stood angrily and declared, "But Glotón will not die! I will kill those that try to kill us!"

Eli frowned, casually reached for the coffee pot and picked up the visitor's cup and refilled it, handing it to him. "I do not come to kill anyone. I have always been a friend of the native people wherever I have traveled."

Glotón glared at Eli, looked down at the cup, back to Eli, accepted the cup and sat on the log, breathing heavily, his nostrils flaring and the muscles in his cheeks flexing as he gritted his teeth in anger.

Eli asked, "What has made you so angry today?"

Glotón dropped his eyes, slowly shook his head and looked up at Eli, "My people were attacked by gold-hunters. I was away, but I heard a shot and returned to see two men trying to take my woman. I killed them both, but they had shot another. Now we must move our village, that is why I am here."

"Were those men white men or Mexican?"

"White men, dirty and smell bad."

"How many were there?"

He held up four fingers, ran his finger across his throat to show they were all dead. He glared at Eli, "I should kill you, so you do not tell others."

"You might not find me as easy to kill, and...I could kill you; then where would your woman be without you?" Eli sipped his coffee, looked at Glotón over his cup and let a grin slowly split his face. He looked at the man before him, remembering this was the man the old-timer had told him about, the one that was killing so many prospectors and others. He called him a renegade, but Eli saw only a native in his own land who wanted to be left alone and to keep his homeland safe from intruders that would destroy and kill. "Your village must be small if four men attacked it. Do you have a family or just a woman?"

Glotón finished his coffee and sat the cup aside, looked at Eli and answered, "It is a small village, three families, others have been taken to the reservation. I have my woman and two little ones, a boy and a girl."

"Is that where you got that rifle, from those that attacked your village?" asked Eli, nodding to the Henry repeater.

The man nodded, grinning, "Yes. He did not need it."

"If you get rid of everything, bury the bodies, drive off the horses and get rid of everything else, no one should find you. It doesn't sound like you did anything but protect your family, just like what I'd do." Eli stood, tossed the dregs of the coffee on the fire and said, "I have a long way to go, so I will leave you to your work." He started to the horses and began tightening the girths and putting the pot and cups back in the packs. He turned to look at the man, but he was gone. Lobo had come to his side and Eli looked around, grinned, shook his head and looked at the wolf, "Well boy, guess he didn't like our comp'ny." He stepped aboard his stallion and with a wave of his hand sent Lobo to scout the trail and started back on his way south.

Although Lobo had become an inseparable companion, he had only been with Eli for a couple months. Found as a weanling pup that came into his camp unbidden, the canine had bonded with both Eli and the horses and had become a trusted member of the entourage. He was a big wolf, even though he had not reached his full growth and would probably add another few inches in height and probably another fifty pounds in weight but was not lacking in strength and stamina and had plenty of grit. Eli chuckled as he watched the wolf trot back up the trail to check on his friends and with tongue lolling, grinning ear to ear and tail wagging, he circled the horses and took off in front again, disappearing into the trees and beyond.

The heat of the afternoon was blistering and the shade from the many oak and pines was the only relief from the still day. No wind stirred the leaves or branches, cicadas and crickets sounded their complaints, squirrels were less vocal with their retorts, and the birds had nested in the shade. This was a dry heat, but miserable, nevertheless. Eli had shed even his leather vest, unbuttoning his shirt half-way, stripping off his scarf and stuffing it in the pommel, using his hat as a fan to cool his face and neck as the horses plodded onward.

The trail stayed near the summit of a long ridge bound southeast, but the trail was narrow, and the trees were thick keeping out the bright sun but also any breeze that would be a relief. The sun was lowering in the west and painting the bellies of clouds with shades of orange and gold when he began looking for a campsite. The trail dipped into the head of a long draw and Eli heard the chuckle of water, grinned and nudged Rusty to the sound. They broke from the trees at a level basin of about an acre. A spring came from a rocky outcrop and a little pool beckoned thirsty horses. Eli nudged them close and slipped to the ground as both horses drank long and deep of the cool water. He pushed them away and began stripping their gear, stacking the packs and saddle in the shade of a mountain mahogany. Once they were stripped, both horses had a good roll in the dusty grass and took to the shade. Eli rubbed them down, picketed them, and went to the water for his drink and to fill the coffee pot for later. As he bellied down, he felt a bit of a breeze and relaxed as he thought relief was on its way.

He stood and looked about. They were on a bit of a saddle just below the crest of the ridge, overlooking the valley below that leveled out and stretched to the distant waters of the south end of San Francisco Bay. He reckoned in the two days of travel out of San Francisco, he had covered a little over thirty miles, but he had more than twice that yet to go before he would get to Monterey.

He began to make camp, thinking about getting an early start, maybe even before first light, come morning and travel in the cool of the day. If tomorrow was going to be as hot as today, they would do best by taking to the shade in the heat of the day. He heard a bit of a rumble behind him, turned to look to the south and saw dark clouds laying heavy on the land and felt the breeze picking up against his sweaty face. He raised his eyebrows, grinned, and returned to his work thinking that if a good rain came, tomorrow's travel might be much more pleasant.

He had a small fire started, the coffee pot siding the flames, and some smoked meat in a pot with some potatoes, onions and water to make him a bit of a stew, when he heard the crackle of lightning and stood to look to the south. Thin fingers of lighting crawled across the sky, splitting the dark clouds with rips of blue and white, the brightness bouncing off the bellies of the storm clouds. But Eli saw no wispy curtain beneath the clouds that would tell of rain, only the skeletal fingers of lightning. He breathed deep, looking around, climbed a rocky outcropping for a better view of the mountainside below him and round about his camp. He shook his head, climbed the shoulder of the hill to look at the ridge and the thin line of the trail that split the thick trees.

Returning to his camp, he looked below, searching the long gulley that carried the little spring fed creek to the bottom, searching for any alternative trail, but he saw none. He shook his head as he looked back to the distant storm clouds and began to pray.

CHAPTER 3

FLIGHT

E li stirred the pot, feeling the breeze from the storm to the south, filled his cup with coffee and sat astraddle of the long rock near the fire. He faced to the south and watched the lightning show, shaking his head and sipping his coffee. Below him to the east the hills lowered their timbered shoulders toward the flats that held many rancho land grants with their grand haciendas and walled courtyards with vast lands of hundreds and thousands of acres of fertile fields, some with fruit trees, vineyards, or wide open pastures with cattle and horses. It was the promised land for many, stretching far and wide with lush fields that could grow just about anything. And the country was growing, the Mexicans crowded out most of the natives, Anglo Americans crowding in on the Mexicans, Chinese being imported for cheap labor, and progress was eating up the land. Railroads, like the one from San Francisco to San Jose, were scarring the land and progress was devouring the trees from the mountains, leaving behind bald scars with ragged stumps and wide slashes of clear cuts that would leave the hillsides barren for years to come.

Eli breathed deep, lifting his shoulders with the effort and shook his head as he turned to fill his plate with his mountain man stew. The wind was picking up, the air cool, but it was tainted with the smell of brimstone from the lightning legs of the black monster that was crawling up the hills. He sat back on the rock, set the plate of stew before him and moved away to get his binoculars. With the fading light of dusk, he did not expect to see much, but he was concerned about the path of the electrical storm that appeared to be coming straight north into the Santa Cruz mountains where he was camped.

He lifted the binoculars to look at the distant lightning, hoping to find the misty skirt of rain trailing beneath the clouds, but there was nothing. He lowered the glasses, searching the area and the sudden display of naked skeletal white fingers driving and dancing at the edge of the hills that brought the stench of brimstone and more. With wide eyes, he searched and saw what he hoped not to see, the orange of low flames, hungrily searching for fodder and easily finding dry timber. Of a sudden, the flames licked heavenward, spiraling upwards as each towering ponderosa was consumed, and the fire spread, fingers of flame snaking along the ground, tentacles of orange forcing the shadows and darkness to retreat. He went to the horses and began saddling them, keeping them picketed and watching over his shoulder all the while.

He knew that misdirected flight was as dangerous as waiting too long, but all too often panic drove people and animals to run without any thought of the direction of the fire nor the lay of the land. The top of the ridge was a wide open park, but dry grasses and shrubs would feed the fire as readily as the dry tinder of standing timber. He needed some natural barrier or break that could withstand the wind-driven fire, but the trail he had followed would be useless to stop the advance of the flames. Wide open dry land, roads, water, any area that would starve the ravenous flames would suffice, but nothing was evident.

"Come with us!" growled a voice from the timber. Eli spun around, hand dropping to the butt of his Colt, and saw Glotón push through the timber aboard a big black horse. "My family is here, come with us!"

"Gladly," answered Eli, turning to point at the advancing fire, "that will be climbing the hills soon. We need a break or water or something."

Glotón nodded, "We go!"

Eli nodded, swung aboard the stallion and motioned Lobo alongside and as the big black horse turned away, Rusty was close behind. The grey did not miss a step and was moving as if he were a shadow of the big stallion. The fading light and deep shadows made Eli trust Glotón as they twisted through the black timber. Crossing over the ridge and moving to the west, the last light of dusk made a silhouette of the distant horizon, but the grey skies offered glimpses of the trail they followed.

Glotón had his son riding behind him, and his woman with her daughter had pushed into line behind her man. Eli kept Rusty's nose to the tail of the buckskin mare ridden by the woman as Glotón picked up the pace. He twisted around and called to the others, "We must hurry!"

Eli felt the trail drop into a deep ravine. Thick pines, ponderosa, sugar, Monterey and incense cedar grew close as they climbed the steep hillsides, but the trail took to the bottom of the ravine. A sharp dogleg bend, a switchback and a short climb up the sidehill and Glotón stopped, jumped down, helped his son down and led the group around the shoulder of some manzanita and into a dark maw of a cave. With a broad overhang, it opened into a large cavern with the sound of water splashing.

"Wait!" demanded their leader, and no one moved until the scratch of a lucifer, and the tiny flame spread light around the broad cavern as Glotón lit a resinous knot of a torch and held it high. "There is room for all. There is some wood, but we will need more. There is water," he nodded to the pool that reflected the fire of the torch.

"I will start the fire," stated his woman, motioning to her son and daughter to bring some wood.

Eli said, "There's a dead snag just outside. I'll fetch that." He paused, spoke to the woman, "There's food and pans in the packs," motioning to the packs aboard the grey. She nodded and started for the grey, stopped when she saw the wolf and looked to her man and to Eli, but Eli slapped his leg for Lobo to come with him. The woman's eyes flared, and she looked to the wolf, her children, and back to Eli, and slowly shaking her head, she went to the packs.

The wind was whistling, bending the shadows of the dim lit night. A glance to the heavens showed stars and a half-moon in the west, but the southern skies were dark, with momentary flashes of lightning that splashed the clouds with bursts of light. Lobo had stopped, looking around, lifting his nose high and testing the winds, and from high up the hill opposite the cave, the howl of a wolf sounded. Eli stopped, looked in the direction of the call, glanced to Lobo and watched as the big black lifted his head and gave an answering cry of the wild. Eli grinned, looked at his black furry friend, and shook his head, "If that's a she-wolf, you might be in trouble boy, but you do what you want." He chuckled, and with axe in hand started on the standing snag of a long dead ponderosa.

It took little effort to drop the snag, and he quickly grabbed a big armload of broken branches and started back to the cave. He glanced around but Lobo was gone. He grinned and delivered his armload of wood, returned for another, and the smell of smoke and the glow of fire over the ridge, sent him scurrying into the cave.

Glotón was securing a couple blankets at the entry to the cavern, back from the wide overhang. Eli nodded, "Let me help. This is a good idea, it'll keep out most of the smoke and back away from the overhang, the fire won't get to it. Is there another opening for air?"

"Yes, but the cavern is so big, we could not see it all in many days!" explained Glotón. He frowned as he looked at Eli, "Where is your wolf?"

Eli grinned, "He heard the call of another, probably a she-wolf, and he went lookin'. He's not mine, he just befriended us and stayed with us. He does what he wants, so..." he shrugged and held the blanket for Glotón to secure.

The fire came like the thundering herd of buffalo, roaring and shaking the ground, howling and whistling, snapping and crackling, sounding like the screams of ancient banshees. The children huddled close to their mother and Eli and Glotón, stood, holding back the blankets to see the stampeding herd of flaming nymphets licking and jumping from treetop to treetop. Serpents of flame scurried through the trees, devouring everything in their path. They watched as deer, elk, bear, and more fled before the onslaught, twisting and running rampant through the impenetrable forest.

The smoke billowed and twisted, forcing the two men to drop the blankets and return to the cookfire, showing a brave face so as not to alarm the children and woman. Glotón glanced to Eli, motioned to the woman, "This is Amenacer, Sunrise, and the boy is Tejón, Badger, and the girl is Chotacabras, Nighthawk." He looked proudly at each one and motioned to Eli, "This is Eli." The family looked at Eli and Glotón as if waiting for more, but the father shrugged and added, "His name is Eli, it means nothing," and shrugged, grinning.

Eli thought the boy to be about eight summers, the girl about six. The woman was beautiful with long black hair that had a sheen that showed a myriad of colors. It hung loosely over her shoulders, held back by a beaded band that came from behind her neck and over the top of her brow. Her tunic was beaded across the yoke and a thin line down each sleeve. Her open neckline accented the slits in the long sleeves and fringe hung from each sleeve. She too was barefooted, as were the rest of them. Eli chuckled, "I am pleased to meet all of you," looking from one to the other and looked at Glotón, "and I am honored to be included with your family."

"You showed you are a friend when I came into your camp. It is only right."

Nighthawk was filling the plates when the outside sounds changed, and it was obvious that a thunderstorm had struck, the hissing and clatter of heavy raindrops on the fire made a totally different sound and smell, but it was a good sound. But if the storm was heavy and severe, the damage would only be multiplied, yet the threat of fire was gone and even the horses, tethered to the side in the wider alcove of the cavern, showed relief and had settled down. Eli was surprised when he felt wet fur beside him and looked to see Lobo standing and leaning against his leg. He reached down and stroked his head, "Where you been boy? How'd you get in here?" They had been watching the entry with the blankets, often moving them aside to look outside, but they had not seen Lobo come in from the overhang.

Glotón said, "Maybe he came in from the other side. There is another opening, down near the far creek, but there was much brush."

As they talked, Lobo padded away and into the darkness at the back of the cavern, disappearing into the maze of stalactites and stalagmites. Eli frowned, but accepted a plate of food and sat down, cross-legged to enjoy the feast.

CHAPTER 4

COMPANION

The wind howled without let up well into the night, the storm continued to rage and drench the blackened hillsides, and with restless horses, strange sounds that came from deep within the cavernous maize, those inside the cavern spent a restless night. Eli rolled over expecting to feel Lobo near, but the ground was cold and empty. He lifted his hat from his face, tried to peer into the darkness by the dim light of the glowing coals of the cookfire, expecting to see the orange eyes of the black beast staring back, but he was greeted with darkness and a low moaning howl followed by a strange high pitched screech that came from deep within the bowels of the mountain.

Glotón sat cross-legged, his back to the wall, looking about and when he saw Eli stir, he spoke softly, "I believe those are the voices of the ancients. My people believe they walk the dark places and sing their death songs to warn others."

Eli sat up, "I prefer to believe it's the wind moving through the cavern and whistling among the stalactites.

If you walk through them, strike them with a stick, you'll hear different sounds from each one."

Glotón sat silent, staring at nothing, turned to Eli, "I have been here before, and the remains of the ancients are to be found there," pointing with his chin to the black hole of darkness. "I have found those that wore iron on their heads and chests, even on their legs, but they died with their mouths wide, empty hands clawing at the walls and their long knives still in their belts."

"Sounds like the Spanish Conquistadors that came long ago. They wore steel armor and helmets and brought the early black robes." Eli looked at Glotón, who sat unmoving, and asked, "Your name, and the names of your family, are all in Spanish. And you speak English as well. Do your people no longer use their native tongue, that of the Ohlone or Yokut?"

"My people and many others were made slaves of the black robes and their people. The missions tried to make us all like them, to only speak their tongue, and later the tongue of the Anglo. My people were forbidden to speak anything but Spanish and now do not remember the tongue of our ancients." He lifted his eyes to the curtain of blankets that hung at the mouth of the cave, "The storm has passed." He rose and went to the opening, followed by Eli. He pulled the blankets aside and the dim light of early morning showed shadows upon the land, the cool damp air of the cleansing storm wafted into the cave, bringing the smell of soaked charcoal, mud, and a bit of salt. The wind came from the west and lifted up through the ravines and gullies of the mountains, freshening the remaining woods, beckoning to the cave dwellers to come into the open. But the darkness still hung low on the woods, the few stars that shone through the remaining clouds offered little light, and they were on the west facing slope of the mountains and the sun rising in the east would take its time shedding any light to dispel the darkness.

Eli turned back to the cave, went to his packs and withdrew a candle, lit it from the coals of the cookfire, and with a glance to Glotón, "I'm goin' to have a look. Lobo, my furry friend, headed back this way and I think I'll see if I can find him. It's not like him to stay away all night."

Glotón nodded and stirred the coals of the fire, added some kindling and set about making some coffee and more. He did not watch as Eli disappeared into the maw of the cavern.

The roof of the cave lowered as Eli moved into the dark recesses of the cavern, the walls pushed in, and several formations offered obstacles in his way, but suddenly it opened into a vast cavernous display of stalagmites and stalactites of all shapes and sizes, some joined together to appear as pillars. Higher up, the ceiling stretched almost out of sight of the flickering candlelight, and shadows danced with every step taken. He looked for tracks, but seldom saw any, yet occasionally the dust offered prints and he continued into the innermost parts. As the big cathedral lessened and the darkness ahead beckoned to a smaller opening, he took tentative steps, listening to the dripping of water, the gurgle of a pool moved by something, and as he ducked into the tunnel like formation, he heard a low growl, and a second gruff growl, and silence.

Eli lifted the candle, saw movement to the side, and turned with lifted candle to see Lobo with two other wolves, one appearing to be much younger. Both were grey, the bigger of the two almost white with darker ears, muzzle, feet and tail. Both had been singed, maybe burned, by the fire, but Lobo stood protectively before them. He did not move against Eli, but he did not show the usual open mouth, tongue lolling, smile that he was used to, and Eli did not move.

He spoke softly, "So this is where you disappeared to, huh? Found a couple friends?" As he spoke, the two wolves that Eli thought were probably mother and pup, came to their feet, but cowered behind Lobo in the usual submissive manner, heads down, tails tucked, backs arched, ears pinned, and did not look at Eli direct, moving behind Lobo as the big black watched Eli. "So, what are you gonna do boy? I'm gonna be leaving soon, and I like havin' you with me, but if this is to be your family, well..." he shrugged. He reached out to do as he always did and run his fingers through Lobo's scruff, but the wolf stepped back and Eli paused, dropped his hand and said, "I see. Well boy, it's been good havin' you with me, and if you want to come, you can find us, but ..." he shrugged and turned away, surprised that he was heavy with sadness. He glanced back, but the darkness did not allow another look, and with the candle sputtering, he started back to the camp.

Golden light showed through the gaps of the hanging blankets at the mouth of the cave, Glotón pushed a blanket aside and the glowing bottoms of clouds reflected the rising sun. He reached up to pull down the blankets, the light piercing the darkness of the cave, and turned, smiling, "We will leave after we eat," nodded and walked back to the cookfire where Amanecer awaited.

Eli nodded, went to the pack to replace the stub of a candle and returned to the cookfire. The woman had prepared the meal complete with cornmeal biscuits and strips of broiled venison. They made short work of the meal, all were anxious to be on the trail, and soon led the horses from the cave. When they led the horses from the cave overhang, they stopped to look about. Eli's first thought was a reminder of as a lad when he spilled the inkwell on his father's desk and the black ink flowed across the papers, maps and more to the consternation of his father. But his father looked at him, frowned, and asked, "Did you learn anything?"

Eli dropped his head, mumbled, "Yes father, I'm sorry."

"Then get some rags and help me clean it up."

When he returned, his father had rid his desk of the papers and more, and with rags in hand, father and son began the clean-up. When they did the best they could, Eli looked around and up at his father, "But it still shows black, what can we do?"

His father grinned, "Learn the lesson. It just shows that all mistakes cannot be cleared up, but we *can* learn from them. Sometimes, no matter how hard we work, or how much we want to make things better, there are times when all we can do is look at the scars and remember."

And he would remember this land that had been so green and thick with growth, now showed ragged stumps, spots of muddy soil and jagged rocks that were blackened by fire and soot, and nothing could be done but let the Creator rebuild his handiwork.

Glotón was in the lead, followed by his woman, each with a child behind them, and Eli brought up the rear with his packhorse following close behind. Eli stood in his stirrups and twisted around to look back at the overhang and mouth of the cave, thinking about Lobo, but saw nothing. He dropped into his saddle, and looked past Glotón to the heavy timber, untouched by the fire, that lay below them.

They took a trail that rose to the top of a long ridge where a long stretch of open grassland stretched along the spine of the ridge. Glotón stopped, turned and motioned Eli to come alongside. As he did, the Ohlone warrior pointed southeast along the ridge, "That trail will take you to the stagecoach road and the white man town of Lexington. From there you can follow the road to the great waters, or take any trail that will go south, but stay to the west of the mountains." The west facing slopes were untouched by the fire and the trees stood tall, green and beckoning.

Eli stood in his stirrups looking south where the faint trail split the trees but followed the long ridge. He dropped into the saddle, turned to Glotón, "Thanks my friend. Perhaps we will meet again." He extended his right hand and the two men grasped forearms in the way of the people and with a nod to the woman, a smile for the children, Eli nudged Rusty and with a glance to the grey, started on the trail shown by Glotón. As he neared the trees, he twisted around to wave, but they were gone. He chuckled, made a quick look back up the trail hopeful of seeing a streak of black, but there was nothing. He settled into his seat, paused, and as Rusty turned his head, Eli was certain he heard the lonesome howl of a lone wolf.

The trail held to the top of the ridge, often obscured by the thick growths of manzanita, sage, gooseberry and monkeyflower, but the ancient trail had been impressed on the land eons ago and refused to be overgrown or obliterated, always encouraging the passage of wanderers. Below the crest of the ridge, thick timber with pines and oaks and sycamore flourished and Eli thought that forest would be almost impenetrable, and he held to the trail that soon dropped off the ridge and began to ride the rolling shoulders of the west side and moved toward the bottom of the valley that lay between the ridges but still pointed south.

The ridges petered out, dropped off to wide points and gave way to the road that cut in from the west. Los Gatos creek meandered through the valley to split the ridges and make its way to the San Francisco Bay, but for now it was the sole source of water for the little settlement of Lexington. Eli reined up while still on the trail that shouldered the ridge, leaned on the pommel and looked at the valley below. The town looked like so many in the west, one main street that held the businesses, one or two other streets that showed the homes and more of others. He started to nudge Rusty on but was stopped when he heard the coming of a stage from the east, made evident by the shouts of the driver, "Eeeeyahhh horses, Ándele! Ándele!" followed by the repeated crack of the bullwhip over the heads of the four-up team. The rattle of trace chains and the creak and groan of the stage rocking on its thoroughbraces, were all familiar sounds to Eli and he grinned as he nudged Rusty down the trail to enter the town.

Dust still hung in the air when Eli turned Rusty up the main road of the little settlement of Lexington. Sun bleached clapboard siding showed grey under the overhanging porches that covered much of the boardwalk. A livery with a blacksmith sat back from the road, tucked into the trees with a sizeable corral, both sides of the road showed a saloon, the *Five Aces* on the north, the *Red Parrot* on the south. A general store had a swinging sign that creaked with the wind and was peeling its paint, a red and white barber pole hung outside a small one-window shop, and opposite the livery was a lumber mill, the big saw grinding away to lull the residents to sleep or anger them according to their temperament. A lop eared dog had lifted his head when the stage passed but dropped it between his paws and was already snoozing. Two horses stood hipshot at the hitchrail before the *Red Parrot,* a buckboard with a mis-matched team was sitting in front of the general store, and one man with grey hair sticking out from under a bent top hat rocked in a rocking chair before a painted window that said, *Undertaker - dentist - attorney.*

Eli chuckled and reined up in front of the general store, behind the buckboard, and slapped Rusty's reins around the hitchrail, slipped the lead rope off Grey's neck and did the same. He stepped up on the boardwalk, slapped his hat against his britches and pushed open the door to the store. The smells of leather, kerosene, pickles and more assaulted his senses as he stepped into the dimly lit interior, but he was greeted with, "Howdy friend! Come right on in an' look around. Be with you shortly!"

CHAPTER 5

REDWOODS

Eli stepped to the counter, put his scribbled list on the top and looked at the man in the long canvas apron, "Fill it if you can, please. I'll look around while I wait."

"Certainly sir," began the merchant, adjusting his glasses to read the list, then look over the rim at Eli, "Will this be all?"

"Prob'ly, but I've got a couple questions for you," he reached into his vest pocket to extract the ever-present tintype to lay it on the counter, "Ever see those two before?"

The man picked up the tintype, held it close and frowned, "You a lawman?"

"No, those are my sons, and as you can see they're twins. I've been looking for them for a while and the last I heard, they jumped ship in San Francisco and were reported to be riding south toward Monterey. Thought they might have come through here. Seen 'em?" he asked, nodding to the tintype in the man's hands.

"Dunno, they look kinda familiar, especially bein' twins, but I just don't recall when."

"Mighta been more'n a couple weeks back," offered Eli.

"Yeah, yeah, now that you say that, I think I mighta seen 'em. They was low on supplies, and they bought a couple rifles too. Had a couple Henrys, and they bought them. Yeah, that was them, cuz I remember thinkin' they looked alike and was gonna be armed alike," he chuckled. He looked at Eli, handed back the tintype, "I'll fill that order for ya."

"Did they say anything, you know, like where they were going or..." he shrugged, looking at the storekeeper and hoping for an answer.

"Mister, that was quite a while back, an' I figger I was doin' good just rememberin' they was here." He paused, put his hand to his chin and stared at the glare from the window, looked back at Eli, "Nope, can't 'member nuthin'! But most folks follow the stage road outta the mountains, down to Santa Cruz and if'n they's wantin' to go further south, most of 'em takes one o' the trails what cuts off'n the road," he shrugged and went about gathering the goods for the order.

————

ELI WATCHED THE STAGE, now with a six-up pulling, stretch out from the stage station and noticed it was loaded, with folks at each of the windows and three up top with the excess luggage. He knew most Concord stages were set up with three rows of seating inside and could carry nine passengers but often some daring passengers would ride up top behind the driver and messenger. Not only would the six-up have a steady pull uphill, but they would also have a full load dragging behind them.

Eli chuckled, nudged Rusty to the edge of the road and the grey followed close behind. The storekeeper suggested Eli stop in the little settlement of Highland, where the stage would also change teams, and ask the man in the mercantile if he had seen his boys, although after supplying in Lexington, they probably would not stop again until further down the trail. The shopkeeper added, "Course, if'n they weren't gonna foller the stage road, that'd be where they'd cut off and head east toward the end o' the hills and on to Monterey."

But Highland gave Eli no new leads and he took the trail to the southeast that headed into the thicker timber. The smithy at the livery suggested he take a lesser known trail that sided the long ridge, "It cuts through the thicker timber where the redwoods are, but it sides the long ridge. It's a good trail, ancient one used by the natives, most folks don' know 'bout it, but that's the way I go when I don' wanna go to Santa Cruz. There's anoth-er'n up top o' the ridge, but it's longer by 'bout five, six miles."

Eli preferred the lesser trails, being a solitary man and enjoying his traveling time alone when he could spend a little more time with his Lord. He enjoyed talking to God out loud and if folks were around, they might think him a little daft. He chuckled to himself and nudged Rusty to pick up the pace a little. Eli twisted around in the saddle to look at his back trail, hoping to maybe see Lobo, but there was nothing but shadows behind him.

The trail broke from the thick timber but sided a steep hill almost like an eyebrow trail, the embankment dropping away into a deep, narrow ravine off Eli's right shoulder. The timber across the ravine was thick and dark, showing the tall ponderosa that were dwarfed by the nearby redwoods. Narrow crowned firs were thick, but the redwoods were crowding out most of the lesser trees, towering high above with their conical crowns. The trail broke into the open with the steep, rocky slope stretching above with its chaparral coat of a variety of brush, some, like the monkeyflower, showing little yellow blossoms to add splashes of color to the hillside. Eli noticed some sugarbush and manzanita and started to twist in his saddle for a better look at what he thought was yarrow, but a sudden jolt dropped Rusty to his knees and unseated Eli as he tumbled over Rusty's head.

Landing on his shoulder, Eli kept a grip on the reins and jumped to his feet, looking around wide-eyed. Rusty struggled to his feet, ears pricked, nostrils flaring and let loose a low nicker as he turned to see Grey crowding close behind. Both horses stood spread-legged, trying to keep their footing. Eli leaned against the big stallion as he looked at the steep hillside before them. A big part of the shoulder slipped, slid and started down the hill, carrying the brush, sage and rocks with it, but many of the bigger boulders had already started tumbling down the steep slope. Eli jerked Rusty's head around, "C'mon boy, back to the trees," and he leaned forward, pulling on the reluctant but frightened stallion. Every step was uncertain, and when the ground dropped out from under them, man and horses both went to the ground.

Eli crashed down on his shoulder, still gripping the reins, and struggled to his feet, the ground continuing to shake. The air was filled with the cracking of timber snapping off, breaking solid trunks and tops tumbling down, breaking branches as they fell. The hillside moved, but where the bigger trees stood, they shook as if held in the hands of an unknown giant that was shaking them as a child would shake a stick. Eli pulled and tugged, coaxed, and shouted, as he gripped the reins in white-knuckled hands, begging Rusty, who stood with front legs spread, rump dropped and hind legs digging in and plowing the trail.

But it was the grey that pushed past the reluctant claybank, trotting on uncertain footing, heading for the dark timber that looked like a refuge. When the grey nickered, turning back to look at his stallion friend, Rusty rose up and almost dropped Eli to his haunches when the reins slacked, but both man and horse turned to the trail and started after the mountain bred and raised mustang.

The trees were still shaking, elm, oak, and more losing branches that snapped off, pines and junipers losing cones and limbs. The few rocks that had been held in place by nearby trees, uprooted trees and soil and both crashed down the steep slopes but only until meeting a cluster of stronger, better rooted trees. Three blacktail deer were running through the trees, jumping and bouncing, driven by their fear and more. Birds had left their perches and nests and took flight, a circling eagle screamed as if warning other animals in the woods. Trees groaned, scraped against one another, and dust rose like a vaporous cloud coming from the soil that had been moistened by recent rains, but still it came.

Eli was afraid to stand near anything, rocks, embankments, trees, and more that had been such stabilizing features, now were unsafe and even frightening. He felt his heart beating as if it wanted to escape his chest, his head throbbed, and his breathing came in gasps. He stayed at the head of the stallion, rubbing his head and neck, reaching out to touch and reassure the grey, but he was uncertain whether he was comforting them, or they were reassuring him. The shaking, rolling, and tumbling seemed to last for a long time, but Eli knew it was just a few minutes. The trees stilled, the ground no longer pitched, the only sounds were of loosened rocks that tumbled downhill, crashing into the brush and trees and more.

Finally everything was quiet, but Eli's breathing was still labored, his heart throbbing in his chest, and he tried taking deep breaths, felt Rusty push his face against his chest, and he stroked the big stallion's cheeks and neck, "That's muh boy, easy now, I think it's over," and reached for the grey who also rubbed his head against Eli's shoulder.

Eli led the horses from the trees and along the trail, slowly and carefully with each step, but all was still and only the occasional loosened stone would give way and roll yet causing enough alarm for both man and horse to look and watch. The shoulder of the slope had slid in one big slice, shifting what Eli estimated to be a good six feet, obliterating the trail, but they had to cross so Eli stepped tentatively on the loosened soil and often bending to reach out with his hand to steady his move-ment, yet the horses, trembling and uncertain, followed at his tugging and encouragement. It was a stretch of about thirty yards, and even though each step was on loosened soil, they made it across the slope, and found certain footing on the trail just before it re-entered the thicker timber.

They stopped, Eli breathing heavily, and with a chuckle he put his forehead against the face of Rusty and stroked his cheeks and neck, "We made it boy, we made it. Now, let's get a move on and see if we can get outta these hills 'fore they start shakin' again." He stepped around, stuffed his foot in the stirrup and swung aboard. Grey moved closed, rubbed his nose on Eli's leg and the trio started back on the trail.

The trail rode the hillside above what Eli would learn later was Soquel Creek and broke from the trees late in the afternoon. Eli reined up, stood in his stirrups and looked across the flanks of the hills and on to the fertile green flats, spotting a few farms and fields with farm-houses and outbuildings, and off on his right alongside a meandering river that emptied into the bay, a bit of a village or settlement. Eli spoke aloud, "That must be what the storekeeper said was what they're callin' Watsonville. Reckon if they got a livery and maybe a hotel, we might just stay the night there, what say, boys?"

"Wal, we ain't yore boys, but we're thinkin' 'bout spendin' the night there too!" came a voice from just past a cluster of trees where another wisp of a trail came from a long ravine that sided a finger ridge that had paralleled the trail ridden by Eli.

Eli leaned both hands on the pommel of his saddle and watched as two riders came from behind the trees, both with floppy hats, baggy britches, and dirty faces and riding what appeared to be a matched pair of mules. But neither had whiskers and Eli frowned, giving the two the once over, trying to determine if they were men or women.

CHAPTER 6

CHANGE

The raspy voiced speaker grinned, pushed the floppy felt hat back to look at Eli and asked, "Mind if we ride along with you? We're goin' to that town yonder, an' like you said, mebbe spend the night there and go on to Monterey in the mawnin'."

Eli nodded, grinning, "I'm Elijah McCain, and I'd welcome the company. As you heard, I've been talkin' to my horses a good spell now and they're not much for conversation."

"Hehehe, I hear ya'! I'm Maude Watkins," putting her finger to her chest, and waving it back, "That there's muh daughter, Mattie."

Eli touched the brim of his hat, nodded, "Pleased to meet you ladies."

"Go 'head on, lead off an' we'll foller," directed Maude, as she slapped legs to her mule with a "Come on, Meg, foller that feller!"

———

THERE WAS nothing impressive about the town that some were calling Watsonville, after one of the founders, John H. Watson. The town was settled on the site of the Rancho Bolsa Del Pajaro and sat on the banks of the Rio del Pajaro. At first glance Eli guessed there to be five or six buildings on the main road, with a few houses and cabins set back into the trees that lined the river. Standing alone was an impressive two story adobe hacienda that he would learn later was the main home of the rancho. The largest building was a two story clapboard with an overhanging deck that shaded the board-walk. A long sign was hanging on the corner and identified it as the Belle Fontaine hotel and café. Beside the hotel was a barber shop with its red and white pole, and a sign that told of both the barber and bath house. Facing the hotel was a tavern and a general store and a livery that was offset at the end of the street. Eli nodded to the hotel, "I'm gettin' a room, then I'll take my animals to the livery. If you ladies would like, we can have supper together after we get settled."

"Wal, that sounds plum nice, Eli," declared Maude as she pulled a big watch from her pants pocket. "How's-about we meet you in the café 'bout six? That'll give us time to freshen up a mite," she cackled as she grinned at Eli.

For the first time he noticed she was missing most of her teeth and what she had was stained by tobacco, something he expected to see in a man, but not a woman. She had an overall frumpy and dirty appearance, scraggly hair with a touch of grey hanging from under the floppy hat, and her figure resembled a bag of pota-toes more than a woman. She had a red bulb for a nose, a single brow that covered both eyes with bushes that made him think of the sage on the prairie flats and when she laughed, her chin almost touched the end of her nose, but her eyes were bright and sparkled with mischief. The daughter showed little resemblance to her mother, but Eli thought she was so skinny she would have to stand twice in the same place just to cast a shadow. Her hair was tucked under the felt hat that was pulled down so far as to make wings out of her ears, and her neck resembled an aspen sapling, with as many spots and scars.

Eli glanced away, looking at the hotel, and back, "Six would be fine."

The hotel clerk frowned when they walked up to the counter and Eli spoke, "We need a couple rooms for one night."

"Yessir, but we do have a big room that might be suitable for your family, sir."

Eli grinned, "No, I need a room, and the ladies need a room."

Maude interjected, "An' we'll be needin' a bath. You got a separate room fer that, or do we get one o' them fancy tubs in the room?"

The clerk frowned, looking from Eli to the women and as his nose wrinkled and his nostrils flared, Eli could tell he agreed that the women needed a bath. Eli dropped his head to hide his own grin and keep from laughing, but the clerk answered, "Yes ma'am, we have a separate room for that, it's right at the end of the hall and I'll have the girl get the bath ready for you. Will that be one or two?"

Maude frowned, "Cain't you count sonny? There's two of us!" motioning to her daughter and to herself as she scowled at the man.

"Yes'm, two it will be," he answered, looking from Maude to Eli and down to his register.

AFTER A SHAVE, haircut, and a bath at the barber's place, Eli returned to the hotel looking and feeling like a new man. When he stepped into the café, he looked around, but the women had yet to come down and he took a table near the window and ordered some coffee to enjoy while he waited. The café was busy with most tables taken, and two long tables that accommodated at least eight to ten diners each, a common sight where there were many single men.

He was looking out the window at the tavern and general store across the road, saw several horses standing hipshot at the rail before the tavern, a buckboard in front of the general store, and a rocking chair on the boardwalk in front of the store with a dozing oldster and a lop eared dog snoozing at his feet. A general murmur brought his attention back to the café and looked at the doorway that opened to the lobby of the hotel and saw two women, smiling in his direction, but he did not recognize the two, until the older woman raised a hand and waved, smiled an almost toothless smile and started in his direction. Eli was surprised at the transformation in the two, both with attractive but simple dresses, their hair done up with Maude having a bun at the back of her head, a wisp of a curl hanging down on either side, the touch of grey he had seen before now shone like a braid of silver. Her dress was a dark blue with lace at the collar and sleeves, and down the front with a belt of white. The full skirt had a thin line of lace at the hem and the lace up shoes showed their toes at the hems edge.

Mattie's hair hung in long curls to her shoulders, a light touch of rouge and lip color accented her smiling face and sparkling eyes showed the same mischief as her mother's. Her dress was a gingham check with buttons down the front, a plain white collar, and matching belt and reticule. She was simply attired, but with her wide smile and dancing eyes, she attracted the attention of all the men sitting at the long tables, and Eli noticed three men at a small table that gave a more than interested look at the pair.

The two women walked directly to Eli's table, and he held the chairs for them to be seated, seated himself and said, "You ladies look very nice this evening. I've taken the liberty to order for you and our server will be back shortly."

"Why thank you, Eli. You look quite handsome your own self," chuckled Maude.

Eli grinned, glanced about the room and told Mattie, "And you, Mattie, have attracted the attention of most of the men in here," nodding toward the long tables where several, young and old alike, of the men were still looking at the ladies and the one man seated with them. He guessed they were thinking he was her father and were hesitant to make an advance. But his attention was taken by Maude when she said, "Well, she might have their attention, but we ain't interested in no romance right yet, are we girl?" Mattie dropped her eyes, smiling, but answered quietly, "No mother."

Maude looked at Eli, "Are you goin' on to Monterey in the mornin'?"

"Yes'm. Planning on pulling out at first light. What about you? Are you staying here?"

"No, we need to go to Monterey also. There's a good assay office there an' we need some ore assayed and," she paused, looking around to see if anyone was listening, lowered her voice and leaned closer, "An' we need to deposit some gold in the bank there." She leaned back, "So, if'n you wouldn't mind, we'd kinda like to travel along with you, you know, ain't too safe for two good lookin' wimmen like us'ns to be travelin' alone," she giggled as she held the napkin to her face and looked at Eli wide-eyed.

"I understand." He also noticed the three men at the table nearby and thought they might have over-heard what Maude said, as they turned to one another, heads down and leaning close, with one man nodding toward the table with the ladies as they talked together in low tones. Eli spoke a little louder than Maude, "And yes, it would be good for us to travel together. Monterey is less that a full day's ride so we should do alright."

———

FIRST LIGHT as the slow rising sun began painting the cloudy sky with a broad brush of orange and pink, the three rode from the livery, Eli in the lead with the grey packhorse following close behind, keeping his distance from the two recalcitrant mules ridden by the women. They had swapped their dresses for their road attire, baggy britches, homespun shirts, floppy hats, thinking they could pass for men, but their clean faces, broad smiles, and chattering manner would make a lie of their pretense.

When they cleared the flats south of the river and entered the trees, mostly juniper with some oak and cottonwoods that sided the little creek, Eli reined up and as the women came close, he asked, "Are you ladies armed?"

"Why?" demanded Maude, frowning and cocking her

head slightly as she looked at Eli, wondering if her trust was unwarranted.

Eli leaned on his pommel as he began, "There were a few of those men in the café last evening that showed a little more than expected interest. I think they heard you talking about the assayer, ore and depositing gold in the bank."

"You 'spectin' them to try to take it from us on the road some'eres about?"

"Ummhmm."

Maude twisted around in her saddle and bent down to withdraw her weapon from the scabbard, prompting Mattie to do the same. Maude lay a double barreled coach shotgun across the pommel, and patted her pocket to indicate she had more shells ready. Mattie lay a Henry .44 across her pommel and grinned as she looked at Eli.

Eli chuckled, stepped down and went to the packs to retrieve his Colt revolver shotgun. Stepping back aboard, he did as the women and lay the weapon across the pommel of his saddle, nodded to the ladies and nudged Rusty back to the trail. The sun warmed their left shoulders whenever it could pierce the branches of the trees but when the trail left the little creek and joined the stage road on the flats of the wide shoulder, the dust rose with every footfall and the heat of the day began to give warning of what was to come.

CHAPTER 7

CONFRONTATION

I t was known as the Devereaux House, although it had been the home of the Reverend Walter Colton, the first American Alcalde of Monterey, before he built the Colton House. Purchased by John Robert Devereaux after he made his fortune in the gold rush of '49, the Devereaux family made it their home and Geneviéve was almost immediately accepted in the social circle of the leaders of Monterey. The home was next to the House of Four Winds and around the corner from the Larkin home. The area had become the prestigious address of the community.

With the main structure of two stories, a wide portico faced the front of Calle Principal. An adobe Spanish Colonial style with white plastered walls and tile roofing, it was a spacious and palatial home. The family was gathered in the dining room, seated around the long table with

Geneviéve at the head. As the Chinese woman, whose husband was the household cook, served, Mrs. Devereaux looked at the two couples, surveying what she saw in the young men and her daughters. She looked at the four and said, "Let me tell you about my husband, John Robert Devereaux." She folded her hands together and looked around the table as she began, "John was a hardworking man, always thinking about his family and determined to provide for us. When he heard about the rush of '49, he immediately set out to make his fortune. He was lucky, he had an exceptional claim and he worked it night and day. He had two partners and after he made a good stake, he bought them out and it was after he had sole possession that he made the big strike. His goal was to take out five tons of gold, but the claim petered out when he broke four. He banked his riches, and after setting us up," she motioned around at the furnishings and the home, "he was determined to make the fifth ton and maybe more. That's why he headed north to the Montana strike, bound for Bear Gulch. But he died just outside Walla Walla, Washington. However, he did leave his family well provided for, as you can see."

She leaned forward and picked up the goblet of water and took a sip. "You see, my girls have never known poverty. They were quite young when we came to this land, and they were infants when my husband made his fortune. All they have known is a life of comfort and luxury, although I did my best to teach them to be strong and willing to work if necessary, but it has not been necessary." She paused and waited for Xīn yán to place each filled plate before those at the table. When the woman left, she motioned for them to eat, but continued, "You have implied that both of you want to marry my daughters," and saw the wide looks the four young people gave her as if a great secret was out, but she waved off their objections and continued, "yet you have no means of support, no prospects of making a living and supporting my daughters in the manner they have known all their lives."

She paused and picked up her fork and began nibbling at her food, continually looking at the four young people before her. "Jubal, tell me about your father. All we know is that he was a soldier. What kind of father was he and did he take care of your mother and you boys as children?"

Jubal looked up at Mrs. Devereaux, lifted his napkin to his lips after setting it down, began, "He is our step-father. Our father died before we were born, and he elicited a promise from our step-father to take care of his wife, our mother, and he agreed. But he and our father were classmates at West Point, and both were committed to the military. We saw very little of our step-father, he was stationed out west before the war, and then, of course, there was the war. We were raised by our mother and our grandparents. They have a large horse farm in Kentucky. We never wanted for anything in our growing-up years and our mother wanted us to go to university, but the war interfered in that. We thought it would be best for us to join the army, like all the other men our age were doing, and left home to join up. But, well, army life was not for us and at the first opportunity, we left, returned home, said our goodbyes and headed to the gold fields in Montana territory, looking to make our fortune, much like your husband."

"And did you?" asked the woman.

"We worked at it, made a little color, but saw more money being made by those that were mining the miners, so we joined up with a pack train, worked on a river boat, were shanghaied, and ..." shrugged Jubal, grinning.

"And what are your plans now?"

"We," began Jubal, looking at his brother and the two girls, "need to take some time and decide about that. What we do know," he nodded to his brother, "is that we love your daughters, and we would not want to fail them in any way, or you, Mrs. Devereaux, and nothing will be done until we have a suitable plan, at the very least, and with your permission, those plans will include Gabrielle and Gisèle."

"That is all I ask, gentlemen. There is no hurry, and if I can be of help, please allow me that privilege."

"Certainly, ma'am."

––––––––

THE SMITHY at the livery in Watsonville suggested they take the stage road through the hills, "Course you could take the slough road, but if'n it comes a rain, you might not make it out!" But Eli usually preferred the hill country and the cover of trees. The road stayed in the draw between the two stretches of timber covered hills, a valley some had called the San Miguel Canyon, but compared to the canyons he traveled in the Rockies and the Cascades, this was just a draw or long ravine. He was also skeptical as to the possible highwaymen from the café at the hotel in Watsonville, for he and the women had left at first light and most ne'er do well outlaws are not early risers. But it was always best to be prepared.

When the shoulders of the hills pushed in on them and the rise to the east showed thick chapparal and the hills on the west were thick with black timber, Eli reined up, let the women come alongside. He looked at Maude, "I dunno, I got that creepin' feelin' up my backbone that has never failed me, but..." he stood in his stirrups, trying to look through the timber and further up the road, but nothing showed danger. He dropped into his saddle, looked at the two, "If anybody comes, from any direction, I'm thinkin' there will be three of 'em, the three that sat at the table near us in the café. And when they do, I'll take whoever's in the lead, Maude you come this side," motioning to his right, "and take the one facing you. Mattie, you do the same on this other side, and as soon as we stop, bring your weapons to full cock and don't be afraid to let 'em hear it. If any of 'em tries anything, don't hesitate to shoot." He looked from Maude to Mattie, asked, "Got it?"

"Yup," declared the women in unison, which caused them both to chuckle and grin.

Eli grinned and said, "Alright, let's go," and nudged the stallion onward.

They had ridden a little more than five miles from the town of Watsonville when the road split the timber, timber that stood high and thick with ponderosa, spruce, and some redwoods, all with long shadows and the sun that had warmed their shoulders before, had hidden itself behind the thick timber. The bend in the road before them whispered a warning to Eli and he glanced to the two women, nodded and lifted his Colt shotgun to rest the butt on his thigh, barrel pointed skyward. As the road bent to the west around the dog-leg bend and the trees stepped back, the three men sat their horses in the middle of the road, grinning as the three travelers showed. But Eli noticed the change in expressions when they saw the weapons at the ready and the black bearded one lifted a hand and greeted them, "Wal, howdy folks! Din't 'spect to see nobody on the road this early in the mornin'."

"That why you left town so early so you could do your deed 'fore anybody else came along?" asked Eli, cocking the hammer on the shotgun and letting Rusty keep walking toward the three. He could tell the women were close, the heads of the mules beside the flanks of his mount. They did as Eli had said and cocked the hammers on their weapons, the racketing of the hammers sounding loud in the trees. Eli whispered to the women, "Both the others have their pistols down by their legs."

The talker kept his hand up, palm forward as if stopping them and said, "Whoa on there! We mean you no harm. Why the guns?"

"Just in case we see any varmints or game, you know, like skunks, buzzards, the like."

"But all we was gonna do was lighten yore load a mite, you know," as he spoke he slowly lowered his hand, grinning and looking wide-eyed to appear friendly, "Since we'ns are genna'men we thought we'd take that heavy load off'n yore hands, sorta make your travelin' easier, ya' know what I mean?" As he talked about the load, his face turned ugly and his nostrils flared, his voice growled as he grabbed for the pistol in his belt which prompted the others to lift their pistols, but the timber roared with gunshots and lead split the air as the shadows were parted with the grey cloud of gunsmoke. Two shotguns roared and spat multiple .30 caliber balls as the Henry bucked and spat the .44 caliber ball. The face and neck of the talker was churned into ripped flesh and splattered with blood and the man's face was obliterated, the man's body lay back over the cantle of his saddle and rolled to the ground. The second and younger man before Maude took the buckshot from both barrels in the chest and the shot spread from one arm to the other and tore away the man's jacket, shirt, and chest, lifted him from the saddle and dropped him behind his horse. The smaller of the three had faced Mattie but the .44 slug from her Henry ripped through his throat and shattered the neckbone as it tore its way through the thick muscles. The man's chin fell to his chest and the body slid to the side to drop to the ground. At the first blast,'the three horses spooked, reared up, stretched their necks and heads high pulling at the bits in their mouths and the reins gripped in the riders' hands, but when their front feet found the ground, they spun on their heels and took off at a run, away from the melee. The last man that fell still had his foot in the stirrup and was dragged down the road, bouncing and flopping behind an already panicked horse.

Eli and the women sat silent, holding the taut reins of their mounts that had been startled as well, and continued talking softly to the animals, settling them down and keeping them steady. Eli lay the Colt shotgun across his pommel and bent forward to stroke Rusty's neck while pulling the lead of the grey to bring him close as well. The women were one with their mules and all the animals calmed and sat still while the three looked at one another.

"You ladies alright?" asked Eli.

Maude let a nervous laugh come forth and she shook her head, "I think so," she looked across the road to her daughter, Mattie, "How 'bout'chu girl?"

Mattie breathed deep, slowly shook her head, "Don't rightly know. Ain't never kilt a man before."

CHAPTER 8

MONTEREY

This was the land of historic Spanish and Mexican Land Grant ranchos. The stage road ridden by Eli and the women wound through the hills and into the flats that held ranchos shoulder to shoulder and passage was only allowed on the designated road. Some of the ranchos were marked by fences or plastered adobe walls that adjoined the main home. The ranchos, most dating to the mid 1700's, were several hundred acres in size, others in the thousands. When the road broke from the valley, a carved wooden sign marked the boundary of the Rancho Los Carneros but within a short distance, another marked the boundary of the Rancho Bolsa Nueva y Moro Cojo. Vast fields that were fenced and cross fenced held hundreds of cattle and almost as many horses. Eli reined up and sat with hands crossed on the pommel of his saddle and marveled at the herds and the vast stretches of fertile land.

And the scene repeated itself time and again as they continued their southwest trek. Some Ranchos were marked by the whitewashed adobe walls and arching signs hanging over the entry gate, while others used nothing more than carved signs that marked the boundaries or direction to the main hacienda. Eli assumed the size of the ranchos were known by the nearness of the signs and although it was several miles across the Rancho Bolsa Nueva y Moro Cojo, the Bolsa de Escarpines was a brief passage as was the Santa Rita Ranch. He rightly assumed the road took them over the corners of several ranchos when they soon came to the Rincon De Las Salinas. But it appeared every rancho was well stocked with cattle and sizable horse herds. He grinned at the thought of a handful of Vaqueros trying to break and train hundreds of horses, and with his experience with raising horses and his time in the cavalry, he knew it would be a considerable and full-time task. As they passed the many herds, Eli could see what he thought were horses with the bloodlines of Andalusian and other known breeds imported by the Spanish and Mexican landowners. He had always admired the build and conformation of the Andalusian breed but there were other influences involved in these herds and he could not help but think of the times the cavalry was hard-pressed for remounts and thought these herds would be an excellent source to meet just such a need.

It was late afternoon when the road offered a view of the Monterey Bay and the white sails of ships and the cresting white waves lapping at the sandy beaches beyond the rolling hills of dunes. Long grey bellied clouds and mist hung like a curtain in the distance, but the narrow Point Pinos lay like the dark line of destiny pointing the way to the ocean beyond. The road they traveled split, and they chose the southernmost branch that would take them into Monterey from the south where they would be on the high ground and over-looking the historic settlement.

When Eli reined up at the break in the trees where the road from the south dropped off the crest of the hill, they were overlooking the town of Monterey below them and the Monterey Bay beyond. Wooden fingers extended into the water and ships, both steamers and sail, were docked at the many wharfs, gently rocking in the waves in a motion that was mesmerizing to the onlooker. The women came alongside Eli and Maude pointed, "Out yonder near the water is the Custom House an' the assay office is right near and so's the bank. It's called the National Bank o' Monterey. Course there's an office of a feller we been to 'fore, he buys gold dust an' such, name o' Polk."

"So, you want to go there right away, or you gonna wait till mornin'?" asked Eli.

"Wal, if'n you don' mind, I'se thinkin' 'bout sleepin' under the trees, keepin' the mules close and take the ore an' such down there come mornin'. Too heavy fer us'ns to pack. Then when we got money in our pockets, we can put the mules in the livery, get us a room at the hotel, and enjoy ourselves a mite," explained Maude. She looked around a bit, turned to Eli and asked, "How 'bout'chu?"

"I was kinda lookin' forward to gettin' a room, have a good meal, and start lookin' for my boys. This is the closest I've been to finding them."

Maude pointed below, "There's a livery down yonder, right 'bout thar, where them two roads git real close. An' there's a place called the French Hotel not too far from there."

"Well, why don't we both get rooms there and come mornin' you can load up one mule and go to the assay office. That way, you can have a good meal and anything else you want."

"Ain't got 'nuff money fer all that. Need to sell muh dust," grumbled Maude, taking a deep breath that lifted her shoulders.

"Well, how 'bout you let me advance you," began Eli, digging in his vest pocket for a coin, "this twenty dollars and that'll be enough to take care of you for a couple days and you can pay me back when you get your bankin' done." He stretched out his hand with the double eagle gold coin and dropped it into her hand.

Maude grinned, "Only if'n you be sure an' let us pay you back, now, y'hear?"

"Of course, Maude, of course. Now," he nudged Rusty to move out on the road, "let's go get us a room and some supper!"

———

THE FRENCH HOTEL was a two story, unimpressive building, much like most of the other structures in this historic town of Spanish, Mexican, and now American influence. Built of Adobe and white plaster, the plain front showed six windows of the second floor, a wide set of double doors sided by a similar number of windows on the ground floor. But the people were friendly, the accommodations satisfactory, and just around the corner was a good restaurant that was highly recommended by the hotel clerk.

Eli had noticed the women straining under the weight of saddle bags on one shoulder and their bedrolls over the other. When he offered to take the saddle bags, he was stunned by the weight, but he tried not to show his surprise, knowing the contents of the bags were the pouches of gold dust. The raw ore for the assayer was still in the packs with the saddles, but Eli guessed the saddle bags to be at least fifty to sixty pounds each. His quick calculation of the weight and the price of gold told Eli he carried about forty thousand in gold dust as he started to climb the stairs to the rooms on the second floor, but he was stopped by the clerk, "Sir, sir! The ladies will be in a room on the first floor. We always require unaccompanied ladies to be on the first floor while all men are quartered on the second."

Eli turned to face the man, frowned and nodded and followed Maude and Mattie to their room at the end of the hall on the first floor. As he stepped into the room, he carefully lowered the saddle bags to the floor, stood up and stretched, rubbing his shoulders, "I see why you wanted to pack those on your mule! Those are heavy!"

Maude grinned, nodding, "And we'll be glad to be rid of them. Will you go with us in the morning?"

"Yes'm. But for now, I'm going to get cleaned up a little and will meet you at the lobby in, oh, one hour?"

They walked together to the restaurant around the corner from the hotel and were greeted by a skeptical host who looked Eli up and down, but smiled at the ladies and ushered the three to a table that was tucked in a corner and out of the way. Eli chuckled as he held the chairs for the ladies and Maude mumbled, "Impertinent little twit ain't he!?"

Eli chuckled again and said, "That's the way it is oftentimes in the civilized world. If that man only knew what he was doing, passing his judgment of others when he is in neither position or power to judge anyone."

"Ain't it so, ain't it so!" declared Maude, scooting a little closer to the table. She lifted the printed menu and began to look it over, shaking her head as she did, "Ain't they got anything that is just cooked and good to eat without all this palaverin' 'bout how it's done an' such?"

"Well, I'm gonna have that second one down the list. That's about as close as they come to steak and potatoes and biscuits."

"Sounds good to me, how'bout'chu Mattie?"

Mattie smiled, nodded, and answered, "That sounds fine to me too."

The meal was tolerable, nothing special, but they enjoyed watching the people even more. Most were well attired and made it a point of looking down their noses at other diners, excepting only those that came to their table to share greetings. There were a few tables where a group of working men, still attired in their soiled work clothes, were enjoying their meal and paying little attention to others. Eli knew these were the backbone of any community although those that put on airs of sophistication thought themselves more important, Eli also knew that any community made up of the society types would soon fail without the working men.

They left the restaurant and walked back to the hotel by the fading light of dusk but enjoying the quiet and cool of the evening. Although some communities had installed gas lights to make the streets safer and extend the business hours, Monterey had yet to follow suit. When they entered the hotel, they were greeted by the clerk who spoke cordially and nodded to the ladies as Eli said his good nights to the women. Eli turned to the clerk and approached the desk, "May I ask you a couple questions?"

"Certainly sir. How may I assist you?"

"I'm looking for a family by the name of Devereaux. A woman and two daughters, I believe. They are said to have a home here in town and I would like to find them."

"And your business with them?" asked the clerk.

Eli stepped closer to the counter, leaned against it with his elbow on the counter and answered, "I do not think that is any of your concern, sir."

"Ah, yes, I see. Then I have no obligation to answer your question, sir."

Eli grinned, looked at the man and leaned a little closer, "*You* are the clerk. *I* am a guest at this hotel, and you are to accommodate me in any way I see fit. Now, as to the Devereaux family, where might I find them."

The clerk leaned away from the counter, coughed and cleared his voice, began to stammer, "I also have an obligation to protect those of our community."

"Does that include yourself?" asked Eli as he casually pulled his vest back to reveal the butt of the Colt pistol.

The clerk's eyes flared, and he stammered again, "But, but, surely you would not…"

"Why not?" asked Eli. "It has been my experience that when someone receives the proper encouragement they become more willing to be accommodating."

The man gritted his teeth, straightened to stand a little taller, and let out a long breath and said, "The Devereaux home is on Calle Principal, just north of the House of Four Winds. If you follow Pearl Street, where the restaurant is, to the west, you will come to Calle Principal. The house is to the left."

"Thank you. Now, that wasn't so hard, was it? Now," he began as he dug the tintype from his vest pocket, "for my next question," he handed the clerk the tintype, "have you seen those two young men?"

"Are *they* in trouble?" asked the clerk, suddenly even more wary of the man before him.

"No, they are my sons. Their names are Jubal and Joshua Paine."

"But you registered as," he pulled the register close, looking at the names, "McCain."

"Yes, my name is McCain. They," nodding to the tintype, "are my stepsons. I've been searching for them for quite some time, and I was told they might be with the Devereaux family or at least visiting them."

The clerk showed a bit of sardonic grin, cocked one eyebrow high and leaned on the counter with both elbows, "And what is it worth to you to find them?"

Eli frowned, "Are you asking for a reward?"

"Well, if it is that important to you, perhaps a reward would make your search easier," suggested the clerk, grinning as he passed the tintype back to Eli.

"What would you consider a sufficient reward for whatever information you may have?"

"Perhaps one hundred dollars?" he shrugged.

Eli reached into his pocket and brought out a twenty-dollar gold piece, "This is what I offer, *if* what you have to say is helpful. But if not, I might take this much pleasure out of your hide!" he growled as he glared with squinted eyes at the man.

The clerk held out his hand for the coin, but Eli shook his head until the man said, "Your sons are near."

Eli dropped the coin into his hand and asked, "How near?"

The clerk grinned, looked at the coin and said, "Their room is across the hall from yours. They are not there but should return soon."

Eli lowered his eyes, forced himself to calm, and looked at the man as he leaned closer. "Do not! Do not! Do not speak of me to them! Not in any way, do you understand?"

"Yessir, certainly sir."

"If I find out different, I will," he slipped the Bowie

knife from the sheath at his back, "peel your hide one strip at a time until you are totally naked of any skin on your body, but you will still live to suffer!"

Eli returned the knife to the sheath, turned on his heel and took the steps two at a time to go to his room and wait for his sons.

CHAPTER 9

REUNION

"Pa! What're you doin' here?" declared a surprised Jubal, holding onto the doorknob as he stood with the door ajar.

Eli shook his head, "Looks like I'm standing in the hallway. You gonna let me in?"

"Uh, sure Pa," replied a humbled Jubal, pulling the door wide open and moving aside, still holding onto the doorknob as he looked back to see Joshua turning from the window to see his father.

"Jubal," greeted Eli, stepping into the room and seeing the second son, "Joshua." He nodded as he moved toward the only chair in the room that sat beside a small table with a bowl and pitcher sitting beside the single lantern that cast the golden glow about the room. He sat down, motioned to the boys to sit on the bed and looked about as they sat anxiously on the edge of the bed.

"You come to take us back?" asked Jubal, his voice unsteady as he pushed himself further back on the bed.

"No, at least not in the way you're thinking."

The boys looked at one another, back to their father

and Joshua said, "But we thought you were after us for deserting, and now you say you're not? I don't understand."

"And how'd you find us?" asked Jubal.

"Son, I've been followin' you two since you were on the *Louella* headin' up the Missouri. And when you jumped ship to join the freighters, go to the gold fields, Last Chance Gulch, Virginia City, Bear Gulch, freighting with Six, riverboat to Astoria, shanghaied in Astoria, and jumping ship from the *Flying Cloud* and now here. You've been busy with all these adventures of yours."

"But we left the *Cloud* in San Francisco, how'd you find us here?" asked Joshua, frowning and showing his consternation.

Eli chuckled, looked from one to the other, "I had a talk with Captain Creesy and his lovely wife, Eleanor. Seems they had sworn out a warrant for the two of you on the Merchant Seaman's Act for jumping ship." He watched as the boys reacted to the possible warrant, but lifted his hand, "No need for concern. I explained to him the Seaman's Act applies only if the sailor is under a signed contract and since you were shanghaied..." he shrugged, grinning.

The boys looked to one another, obviously relieved and looked to their father. "So, if you're not here to take us back to the army, why the long hunt for us?"

Eli dropped his eyes to the floor, looked up at the boys and began to tell them about their mother and the promise he made. "It was her wish that I find you and try to get you to go back to the home place in Kentucky and make it your home. It is a good farm and they've done well raising horses." He paused, letting the boys absorb the news of their mother's passing and more.

"So, now that you've met these young ladies and are obviously taken with them, what are your plans?"

The twins looked at one another and back to their father, "That's the same question Mrs. Devereaux asked us this evening when we were at supper," stated Jubal.

"And what was your answer?"

"That we didn't know, but we, the girls and us, were planning on talking things out and wouldn't do anything without talking with their mother," replied Joshua.

"Have you managed to save any money on your adventures?"

"A little, but not enough for anything in particular. I reckon we thought we'd get jobs doing something, save up…" shrugged Jubal.

"Tell me about Mrs. Devereaux, is she well known, does she have connections? You know, people in places of influence and such like?"

"I think so, they've been here several years. Her husband made his fortune in the gold rush, but he was killed up near Walla Walla, some incident on a river boat. He was headin' for Bear Gulch when it happened. But she is known around and respected. Why do you ask?"

"I've got an idea brewin' that might be something you two could be a part of, but I need to do some inquiring first. Do you know where a telegraph office is here in town?"

"Sure, it's on the next street over past the Devereaux home, that's where most of the businesses are and there's a stage company office that also has a telegraph. Why?" asked Jubal, frowning.

"I need to send a telegram, make an inquiry before I go too far with what I'm thinking."

GENERAL PHILIP SHERIDAN

U.S. ARMY DEPARTMENT OF THE MISSOURI
ST. LOUIS, MISSOURI

GENERAL SHERIDAN,

WE CAN SUPPLY 5-800 HIGH QUALITY REMOUNTS
FOR THE CAVALRY. DELIVERY TO FORT HAYS
EARLY SUMMER, 1868. IF INTERESTED, REPLY
WITH NUMBER WANTED AND PRICE TO BE PAID.

LT. COL. ELIJAH MCCAIN (RET.)
MONTEREY, CALIFORNIA

The telegrapher looked up at Eli, "That's a lot of horses. You fixin' to ship 'em outta here?"

Eli chuckled, "Ships don't sail to Kansas." He looked about, "When you get a reply, have your runner bring it to the French Hotel, if you would, please." He put a ten-dollar gold piece on the counter, "Give your runner the change, please."

"Thank you, sir!" declared the telegrapher, quick to snatch up the coin. "We'll deliver it just as soon as a reply comes, sir."

Eli grinned, nodded, and turned away from the counter. The women, Maude and Mattie, were waiting at the hitchrail outside the Custom House where Eli had found a telegraph office to send his inquiry. Earlier the three had brought the ore and the gold to the assayer and the gold buyer, but now they were bound for the National Bank of Monterey. The gold buyer had given them a bank draft for the pouches of dust and tried to be nonchalant when he asked, "Where'bouts did you ladies get this gold?"

But Maude was a bit abrupt when she answered, "In the mountains! Where ya' 'spect, pilgrim?"

The man chuckled, nodding, and added, "This is high grade dust, and I can pay you full price of $20.67 per ounce and according to my scales, you have one thousand, nine hundred and twenty ounces. Let's see, that comes to $39,686.40!" He shook his head, looked at the women and Eli and said, "That's the biggest single payout I've had! I'll have to give you a bank draft for that amount, but the bank," nodding down the street, "will honor it just like cash. I'm sure you won't want to carry that amount of money on your person."

"Just never mind my person and make out the draft!" declared Maude.

Jerome Polk, the gold buyer grinned and quickly made out the bank draft, blew on it to dry the ink and handed it over to Maude. He pushed a register before her and asked, "Would you please sign this? It's to show I bought your gold, the amount of the dust, and the price, as well as the total paid." He pointed to the figures as he spoke and handed Maude the steel pen with a gold nib to sign, holding his finger on the designated line.

Maude signed on the line, but looked up to Polk and waved the draft, "If this ain'tny good, I'll come back an' take it outta yore hide!"

Polk leaned back, frowning at Maude, "My dear madam, it most certainly is a valid instrument of banking, as you will find when you go to the bank."

The bank was a short walk from the Custom House and when the three entered, they paused to look around and were greeted by a young man seated at a desk near the entry. "How may I assist you folks?"

Eli stepped forward, "These ladies would like to make

a deposit with a bank draft drawn on the account of Mr. Polk."

The young man stood, motioned for the ladies to take a seat beside his desk and introduced himself, "I am Hobart Coryell, I am an assistant teller. Now," he seated himself behind his desk and took up paper and pencil, "what name would you like for the account?"

Maude frowned, glanced from Eli to the young man, "Why, in my name, of course. What other name would I use?" She humphed and crossed her arms, holding tight to the draft.

"And that would be?"

"Maude and Mattie Humphries."

"And the address?"

"Ain't got no address. We live up in the mountains on our claim."

Mattie looked at her mother and to the young man, "But we won't be there much longer, will we ma?"

"Nope. Gonna buy us a house here in town, or mebbe some'eres else."

"Then we'll just put 'General Delivery' for now." He wrote the note on the paper and asked, "And how much would you like to start with? The draft, I mean?"

"All of it! But I reckon you can give us a hunnert dollars to take with." She grinned, glanced to Eli, "Might need some 'walkin' roun' money! hehehehe." She handed the draft to the young man who looked at it, his eyes growing quite large as he looked at the ladies and around the bank, expecting to see someone else.

"Well, well, this is exceptional! I must speak to our manager." He rose, draft in hand, "and you want one hundred dollars in cash, the rest to be deposited?"

"That right, sonny," replied Maude, frowning.

"I'll be right back!" declared the young man, turning

and walking hurriedly to the office at the rear of the bank. He soon returned with an older, distinguished man, behind him. When they neared the desk, Hobart looked at the ladies and back to the older man, "Ladies, this is Mr. Bartholomew Wilkins, the president of the bank."

Wilkins stepped forward, smiling, and nodded to the ladies, "It is a pleasure to meet you both. It will be our pleasure to take care of your funds and to be at your service any time. We pride ourselves in our bank and the services we offer."

"Fine, fine. Where's our money?" asked Maude, looking at the young man.

Hobart handed her a small satchel, opened and gaping. He pointed to the opening, "Your coin of one hundred dollars is there, along with the booklet that tells of your deposit. Whenever you want to make a deposit or withdrawal, please bring that booklet with you and we will accommodate you."

Maude pulled out the booklet, looked it over, nodded her satisfaction, replaced the booklet and fingered through the coins, and looked up at Hobart and Wilkins, "That will be fine, thank you."

———

WHEN THEY EXITED THE BANK, they paused and looked about, Eli asked, "So, what are your plans now?"

Maude chuckled, "Oh, thought we'd look around the town a little, maybe see if we can find a house to buy, then we'll decide what we'll be doin' after that." She paused, looked at Eli, "We wanna thank you for your help, not that we could'na dunnit without'chu, but it made us feel a mite better with you along."

"It was my pleasure. Perhaps we'll see one another again. I'll be staying around town for a while now, since I've found my sons."

"Mighty happy for you 'bout that," declared Maude glancing to her daughter, "too bad they's spoken for!" She chuckled as Mattie dropped her eyes, embarrassed at her mother's remarks.

"Well, we're not sure what we'll be doing, but we'll have time to make plans and preparations for whatever it is that comes our way. So, if you'll be staying at the hotel, be sure to let us know what you'll be doing." He paused and continued, "Right now, I'm going to do a little shopping for some city clothes. I spotted a haberdashery when we walked through town and thought I'd stop there and look around."

Maude grinned, "Aw, I don't think you'd look any better in some o' those city clothes."

Eli grinned, tipped his hat to the ladies and handed off the lead rope of the mule to Maude, nodded as he turned away to cross to the other side of the street and make for the haberdashery. He knew what he wanted and specified such to the clerk/tailor of the store. "I want trousers of grey pinstripe, a waistcoat of grey and black brocade, and a morning coat of black. Three white shirts and two black string ties. Also, I want a three-piece black wool suit and I'll also have a black flat crowned and flat brimmed hat."

The tailor stepped back, surprised to hear a man attired for the wilderness to speak of the fashionable attire of a gentleman. He nodded, "Let me take your measurements and I'll have those ready for you soon."

"I would like the grey and black for this evening, the suit can wait until tomorrow."

"That would be fine sir, and how will you be paying for this?"

"In gold coin, of course. And if you will deliver that to the French Hotel to Elijah McCain, that would be helpful."

"Certainly sir."

Eli walked back to the hotel, thinking all the while, considering his idea of securing remounts for the cavalry. From the time he was first in the cavalry at Fort Laramie, remounts were always a challenge, especially when the natives would make raids for the sole purpose of stealing horses. And throughout the war, remounts were hard to get, and the lack of remounts more often than not was one of the greatest hindrances to the effectiveness of the cavalry. He also knew the stirrings of wars with the plains Indians would make the need for quality remounts even more pressing. But it would take a lot of effort to find, procure, and mount a drive for a herd in the hundreds across the twelve hundred miles of mostly unsettled wilderness. And it would be more than buying the horses, he would need drovers, a cook, chuckwagon, supplies, and more. He shook his head at the thought, but also grinned as he thought of spending that time with his sons and undertaking a task that as far as he knew, had never been done before.

CHAPTER 10

PLANNING

The three men, Eli, Jubal and Joshua, were seated at the table nearest the front window of the restaurant where Eli and the ladies had supper the night before. As they ate, Eli began explaining his idea, "And depending on the price the army will pay, there could be a good profit in it that would give you boys a good nest egg for your future. And since we'll be back in that part of the country, you won't be far from the farm and maybe you could go by there and talk things over with the attorney that's been handling your mother's affairs and if you decide, you could make your home there. That would be a good home for your families."

Jubal looked at his father, glanced to his brother, "We talked about that a little after you left last night. We always liked the farm, and we didn't run away from that, it was just, well, you know, the trouble with the army and us deserting we thought it would be best to be a long way from the farm. It sure won't be the same with Ma gone."

"No, it won't. But if you like farming, raising horses, and such, it could be a good life for you and a good place to raise a family."

"Gosh Pa, we just met up last night and you've already got us married off and havin' kids!" chuckled Joshua, shaking his head as he finished off his meal. He reached for the coffee cup and started to take a drink, but paused, "But it does sound good, a family and all."

Eli grinned, looked the boys over and asked, "Are those your best clothes?"

Jubal looked down at his attire, the gabardine trousers, linen shirt, and drop shoulder jacket, "Yeah, it is. We don't have enough money to spend just on clothes."

Eli grinned, "There's a good haberdashery up the street yonder. I bought some clothes earlier, and it wouldn't hurt for you to do the same. The tailor, Frederick, can get you outfitted a little better." He pushed a double eagle to each of the boys, "In the eyes of many, appearance makes the man. But try to save some for later. If we make this trail drive, we'll be needing something other than city duds."

————

"THAT IS QUITE AN UNDERTAKING, don't you think, Mr. McCain?" asked Mrs. Devereaux as she sat at the head of the table in her dining room. Eli was at the foot of the table and the two couples were seated on either side. When Mrs. Devereaux learned of the sudden appearance of the father of the twins, she insisted they all come to dinner and get better acquainted. When she had inquired as to his plans and the possible plans of the twins, Eli had explained, "I received an answer from

General Sheridan this afternoon. He is willing to contract for eight hundred, give or take, head of remounts for the cavalry. At the going price to be paid upon delivery, it would make a tidy sum for the boys to have to start their lives as family men."

"But, surely that is no easy task, I mean, we are a long way from, where will you take them?" asked Mrs. Devereaux.

"Fort Hays, Kansas. It's about twelve to thirteen hundred miles from here. That would be about a ninety-day trail drive for the herd. And no, it will not be easy. Not only is it a long trail, but it will also take us through some rough country, over the Rocky Mountains, across much of the great plains. Not to mention that much of that country is Indian country."

"Just the three of you?"

Eli chuckled, "No ma'am. We will hire several men, vaquero types, and a cook and helper, perhaps more."

"And where will you get all these horses?" she asked, watching her maid, Xīn yán, serving them as she placed full plates before each one.

"There are many ranchos that have hundreds of horses. I did a little inquiring around and it seems there is no market for horses hereabouts, and not much of a market for cattle. The cattle that are sold are butchered and the fat rendered and the hides, which are called California dollars, are stacked and shipped east. But they can't do that with horses and with a glut of supply, I believe we could put together a herd in short order."

The maid had finished serving, stood back from the table with hands folded before her, waiting for any other instructions. When Mrs. Devereaux started to begin, Eli interrupted, "Ma'am, would it be alright if we asked the Lord's blessing on this fine meal?"

Mrs. Devereaux was visibly taken aback, but nodded as she said, "Of course, you may," and looked at the two couples as she set the example by folding her hands and bowing her head. Eli began with, "Our Gracious Heavenly Father, we thank you for this bountiful meal, the good company, the hospitality of this fine family..." and continued for a short while and concluded with, "...in Jesus name, Amen." As he lifted his head, he reached for his fork and looked at his full plate, nodding and said, "My, this looks wonderful!" He looked at the maid, "My compliments to the chef!"

"Thank you, Mr. McCain. It has been some time since we've had the pleasure of a man at our table, especially one that is prone to prayer," stated Mrs. Devereaux, lifting her napkin from beside the plate and laying it across her lap.

"Please ma'am, I would prefer Eli or Elijah to Mr. McCain. I was never accustomed to mister, spending so much of my adult life in the military, I was usually addressed by my rank. But I much prefer the use of my given name."

"Why, thank you, Eli, but only if you will use my given name, Geneviève," she replied, lifting the napkin to her lips to hide her coy smile.

"Certainly."

She turned to her oldest daughter, Gabrielle and asked, "Have you girls discussed this grand adventure they are about to embark on?"

"Oh yes, Mother. Isn't it exciting? And we hope to take the stage and train to their home in Kentucky to meet them!"

Geneviève frowned, looking at both girls and the twins, then to Eli, "Really? And when did you decide this?"

Gisèle eagerly answered, "Why today, Mother. Surely you did not expect us to stay behind and let them forget about us, did you?"

"Well, no, but…" she was caught speechless as she looked wide-eyed around the table, saw a slight grin split Eli's face and glared at him, "Did you put this fool notion in their heads?"

Eli chuckled as he responded, "No ma'am. I have never said a word to your lovely daughters, other than 'pleased to meet you.'"

"But mother, it's the only way!" pleaded Gabrielle.

Conversation lagged for the rest of the meal and when they had finished, Eli stood, "If you'll excuse me, I think I would like to have a few moments with my sons. Would it be alright if we use the veranda?"

Geneviève nodded, "Of course. And I'll visit with my daughters as well."

The brief respite allowed everyone time to gather their thoughts as they returned to the parlor. Geneviève motioned the men to the chairs opposite as she said, "Please forgive me for my, well, surprise at the remarks of my daughters. I was not prepared for that retort and, well, forgive me, please."

"Of course, and that is totally understandable. And nothing will happen all that soon, it will take some time to put things together," offered Eli as he and the twins sat on the matching armchair and parlor chairs opposite the settee and wing back chair taken by the ladies. "What we plan to do is first, find a suitable place to hold the herd as we buy the mounts. Then we'll contact the different ranchos to begin buying the horses. At the same time, I'll have to locate a suitable wagon and team and find the vaqueros and cook and more."

"Perhaps I can help with that. I know many of the

wives, socially, of the owners of some ranchos, and some attend the same church. I could let them know, have them talk to you, and maybe pass the word along to other owners. For example, I know the Sargent family, three brothers and their wives that own several ranchos and have considerable herds."

"That would be a great help, Geneviève. We would like to get the herd together and be ready to start the drive no later than the first two weeks of March."

"Oh! Well, I was afraid it would be sooner than that, but, well, that gives me time to get used to the idea," declared Geneviève.

"And Mother, we won't be leaving until after that, and besides, you can always come with us. After all, don't you want to see where we'll make our home?"

"Of course dear, but," she looked from her daughters to the boys and back and added, "what about in the meantime? Are you, well, what about. . .weddings?"

Chapter 11

Preparations

The arch over the entry said *Rancho Noche Buena* but Eli saw nothing that spoke of Christmas Eve. The three men rode into the walled compound before the hacienda and were welcomed by a man who greeted them, "Welcome señors, I am Mateo Guiterrez, the majordomo of the rancho. What is it that you want here, señors?"

Eli leaned forward, resting his forearms on the pommel of his saddle, reached up to push his hat back a little and said, "Mornin' Mr. Guiterrez, I am Eli McCain, these are my sons, Jubal and Joshua. We're looking for some pasture we can rent to keep a herd of horses for a couple months before we move them out." He sat up straight, looking around and continued, "I saw some fine fields with tall grass and nothing on them, do you think we might be able to rent them?"

"Please, step down señors, I will send for the owner, José de Puig Monmany, and we will discuss this." He motioned them to the veranda, clapped his hands to summon another man, one that appeared to be a servant, and showed the men to a table with several chairs, motioned for them to be seated and stepped back as another man came from within the home. When he approached, Eli and the twins stood, Eli extending his hand as Mateo began his introduction, "Señors, this is José de Puig Monmany, the owner of this rancho." After the shaking of hands and the sharing of names, the owner motioned the men to be seated.

He looked at Eli, "Am I to understand that you were inquiring about renting some of our pastures?"

"That's right, we need pasture for a herd of horses for a couple months, maybe a little longer. We are procuring a herd to take east for the army, and we'll need a staging area as we buy the stock and ready everything for the trail drive."

"But you do not have the herd as yet?" asked José.

"No, we're just getting started, but we will pay you in advance for at least two months of pasture and as we buy horses, they will be driven here, and we'll leave from here," explained Eli.

"And will you also need housing for your drovers?"

"If you have a bunkhouse or something of the sort, that would be good."

While the men spoke a matronly woman came from the house with a tray and several cups and a sizable pot. She quietly and discreetly filled each cup, sat it before the men and quickly disappeared around the corner of the veranda. The boys looked at the cups, lifted them and smelled the brew and Jubal took a cautious sip of the hot brew and smiled and nodded. Joshua did the same and the two enjoyed their first taste of champurrado. Eli caught their reactions out of the corner of his eye and grinned, knowing the taste of the delicious chocolate drink.

José looked to Mateo and when the majordomo nodded, he turned back to Eli, "I am interested in this possibility. We have about three thousand acres of fine grass, land that has never been turned and has only been used for livestock, but it has not been used this past year and as you can see, it is not in use now. We have considered disposing of the land and have had some interest and offers, but nothing that would prevent what you propose. And we do have two buildings, a bunkhouse and a storehouse, that could also be used." He paused, looking at Eli and back to his manager, "Mateo, you show Mr. McCain around, the pastures and the buildings, while I talk to my wife and her brother. We will settle things when you return."

Mateo stood, nodded, and motioned for Eli and the twins to precede him as they left the veranda. Mateo said, "I will get my horse and we will ride around the pasture and see the buildings as he said."

The land was more than just rolling grassland. Trees of all types from the redwood and ponderosa to the bearberry, sycamore, cedar and oak. North and east boundaries were thickets of chapparal and manzanita and sage as well with a few stretches of scablands, yet overall there were at least two thousand acres of good grass for graze for the horses, all sided by the sandy beaches and the cool breeze from the bay. Eli spotted two streams that would offer fresh water and the open pastures had good fencing. He looked at Mateo, "This would be just what we need. Can we see the bunkhouse and storage now?"

"Of course, señor. May I ask, this trail drive of horses, where to?"

"Fort Hays, Kansas. It is the temporary headquarters

of the Army Department of Missouri that encompasses most of the central plains."

"And do you have all the men you need?"

"No, we do not. Interested?"

"Perhaps, señor, for if this land is to be sold, where would I be?" he shrugged.

"Well, we won't be leaving for a while yet, and if you know of any others, vaqueros, gauchos, charros, anyone that is good with horses, send them our way."

When they returned to the hacienda, José was waiting with his wife, Jaime, and both were ready to complete the deal. Eli had previously had the bank transfer funds from his accounts in Massachusetts and St. Louis, and he made out a bank draft to conclude the deal. "And if it goes a little longer, we'll settle up before we leave."

"That would be fine, señor," responded José.

Before they left, both the majordomo and José suggested other ranchos for them to look for horses and as they rode from the rancho, they were in a jovial mood and Jubal asked, "We goin' back to Monterey or…?"

"You've only been away from the girls a few hours and you already want to go back?" asked Eli, feigning incredulity.

"No, it's not that. The women were having some kind of social get-together so their mother could talk to some of the wives she knew, women that had a place in town whenever they wanted to get away from the ranch. She thought she could make a good contact for us, maybe more," explained Joshua.

"I know, Geneviève told me about it, and yes, we're going back into town. But we need to get started on buying horses and everything else. You two can't spend your time lollygagging with the ladies, this is your dowry we're talking about."

"Dowry?" asked Jubal, "I thought that was something the parents of the bride gave to the couple."

"Well, yeah, but you get the idea. Call it what you want, but if this works out like we hope, it will give you a good foundation for a family."

"So, how much you think, Pa?" asked Joshua.

"Depends on what we can buy the horses for, I'm thinking we should get all we want for ten to twenty dollars a head, and the price given by Sheridan was sixty dollars."

"Whooeee, that will be a nice foundation," declared Jubal.

"If you two would get enough supplies to last you three or four days, then you could make the rounds of the ranchos to the north and east while I go south. Let's see, that would take us through the rest of the week, and we could meet back at the bunkhouse of the Noche Buena. Remember, nothing over five years old, and if you get the chance to talk to any of the vaqueros and such that might be interested in making the drive, we'll pay $100 for the entire drive, no matter how long it takes, and hopefully if won't take more'n three months. There'll be a bonus if we make it sooner and lose less'n 10%."

"Do we pay up front or on delivery?" asked Jubal.

"I'll give you some bank drafts and you can decide, just keep track of how many and who's delivering the horses. Oh, and we could use a good cook and helper. I'll find us a wagon and team."

They stopped at the general mercantile and trader that was in the custom house building and selected their supplies for the buying trip. With just a few days, they could pack it in their haversacks or bedrolls and would have no need of a pack horse. The twins insisted on stopping at the Devereaux home so they could say goodbye to the girls and Eli wanted to know if Geneviève had spoken to any of the wives or others at her after-church morning social.

———

GENEVIÈVE WAS PLEASED to see the men as they reined up in front of her home. She sat on the veranda at a table with another woman and smiled as the men stepped down. She waved them up on the veranda and introduced them to an older woman who sported grey hair and a mischievous grin. "Gentlemen, may I present Maria Antonio Pico de Castro." The three men had doffed their hats and stood respectfully before the ladies and at the introduction, Eli lightly took the outstretched hand of the older woman in his, bent in a slight bow and kissed the hand of the woman and said, "I am Elijah McCain, and I am very pleased and honored to make your acquaintance." He turned slightly and nodded to the twins, "And these are my sons, Jubal and Joshua."

They nodded, gave a slight bow, "And we are honored as well, ma'am," stated Jubal and Joshua added, "Yes ma'am, very honored."

"And I am also, gentlemen. It is very good to meet each of you."

Geneviève smiled and explained, "Maria's husband was the alcalde of Monterey a few years back and she is now a widow and the sole owner of the Rancho Bolsa Nueva y Moro Cojo, the largest rancho in central California." She nodded to the men and motioned for them to be seated on the bench and extra chairs nearby. She continued, "I told Maria a little about your undertaking and she has expressed interest," she nodded to Maria.

"Yes gentlemen. I understand you are procuring some horses to take east for the army as remounts, is that correct?"

"Yes ma'am. Just this morning we made arrangements with the owners of the Rancho Noche Buena to rent their fields and buildings for our staging area. As we build the herd, we'll pasture them there and make all the other preparations for the drive," explained Eli.

"And how many horses do you plan to take?" asked Maria showing a slight grin at the corner of her mouth.

"We would like to get a herd of about eight hundred or so, depending on the market and availability. We can only take horses that are between three and six years old, hopefully broke to ride, but that might not be probable, so we are amenable. Do you have some horses available?"

"That depends on the price, and I know there is little market for horses now, but we would like to trim our herd before they eat everything we have." She paused, looked at each one and back to Eli, "What do you believe the market is now?"

Eli sighed a little, "From all those I spoke to, horses are going for less than cattle, and they are killing cattle for their hides and tallow. But most horses go between ten and twenty dollars."

"I have a few that I can trim the herd with for fifteen dollars a head," she declared, dropping her head a little to look from under her thin eyebrows, giving the look of a scolding grandmother.

"We will take all you can provide for that price, as long as your men deliver them to the Rancho Noche Buena," countered Eli.

The woman smiled, extended her hand and said, "Done!"

"And how many do you expect to deliver?" asked Eli as he stepped forward to seal the deal with a handshake.

"Oh, three hundred, more or less," she grinned, and added, "all broke to ride."

As Geneviève walked the three men to their tethered horses, Eli asked, "Any luck with any of the others?"

"Yes, I visited with the Sargent women, all three were at church this morning and stayed for the social. When I spoke about you men needing horses, they were pleased. One of the ladies, Julie, whose husband is Bradley, said 'We have too many horses and they're crowding out the cattle! I'm certain our men would be glad to sell.'" She smiled, touched Eli's arm and said, "You are to go to see Bradley, he's the youngest but he's the one that first got into ranching when he bought the Rancho Potrero de San Carlos, that's where Bradley Sargent should be, but you might try his office here in town, near the Hotel Monterey, before you leave. He is an attorney, and a very successful one at that. Now they, he and his three brothers, own two or three others, maybe more." She paused, smiling, "If you would like, I could accompany you and introduce you."

CHAPTER 12

GATHER

Eli pulled the buggy up at the front of the office building that sat beside the bank, stepped down and tethered the horse to the rail and helped Geneviève down and gave her his arm as they started to the entry. Once inside, they were offered chairs in an outer office and the young man who ushered them in, nodded and disappeared to summon Mr. Sargent.

Within a few moments, Bradley Sargent walked into the outer office, nodded and greeted Geneviève with a smile, "Mrs. Devereaux, how nice to see you." He turned to Eli and asked, "And you are?"

Eli stood, extended his hand, as Geneviève introduced him, "Bradley, this is a dear friend and the father of the beaus that are courting my daughters, Elijah McCain."

The man frowned, extended his hand, "McCain, McCain, that is a familiar name."

Eli responded, "I understand you are from New Hampshire, is that correct?"

"Yes, yes it is," he answered, still frowning.

Eli let a slight grin paint his face, "My family is from Massachusetts."

Sargent smiled, nodded, "Ah yes, McCain Ship-builders, the same?"

"Yes, my family has been in the shipbuilding business many years."

Sargent took a seat on a chair near the others, leaned forward, elbows on his knees and looked at the two, focusing his attention of the woman and asked, "So, Geneviève, how may I be of help to you?"

She smiled, glanced from Sargent to Eli and said, "I wanted you to meet Eli, and let you know what he and his sons are planning." She nodded to Eli to pick up the conversation.

When Sargent sat back and turned his attention to Eli, he nodded for Eli to continue.

"We are putting together a trail drive to take some horses to General Sheridan for cavalry remounts. We'll be contacting most of the rancho owners and see if we can build a herd of oh, eight hundred to a thousand or so."

"I see, that is interesting. Have you checked around as to the market for horses?"

"I have, and as you probably know, there is not much of a market. Since the war, there is a glut of horses and cattle, and neither are selling very well."

"True, true. We have too many of both and it would be advantageous for us to trim the herds considerably. What are you looking for?"

"Nothing over five years old, preferably broke to ride, no studs or young colts."

"And what do you believe those to be worth?"

"Depends on the quality and number, but we just bought three hundred from Maria de Castro of the Bolsa Nueva y Moro Cojo, all broke and delivered to our holding ranch for fifteen dollars a head."

"I see, hmmm. If my brothers are in agreement, I believe we could deliver two, maybe three hundred for that price."

Eli grinned, "That would certainly be helpful. When will you know?"

"Are you staying with Geneviève?"

"No, we've been at the French Hotel, but we'll be staying at the Noche Buena where we'll be keeping the herd."

"Then I will send word and we'll make arrangements for payment and delivery," stated Sargent, rising and extending his hand. Eli did the same and the men shook hands to seal the deal and parted.

———

IT HAD TAKEN ALMOST six weeks, but Eli grinned as he looked at their compiled list:

- *Rancho Potrero de San Carlos—Bradley Sargent—275*
- *Bolsa Nueva y Moro Cojo—Maria A. Pico de Castro—315*
- *Rancho Santa Rita—Wm. Mendenhall—35*
- *Rancho Los Carneros—Frederick MacDougall—110*
- *Rancho Las Salinas—Espinosa Family—50*
- *Bolsa del Potrero y Moro Cojo—John Cooper—115*
- *Rancho Tularcitos—Andrew Ogletree—160*
- *Rancho El Toro—Charles Wolter—65*

He grinned as he looked over the list and looked at his sons who were happily grinning at the conclusion of the horse buying. Jubal was the first to talk, "So, whaddaya think Pa? Think we have enough?"

"Well, that adds up to a thousand, one hundred twenty-five and at an average price of fourteen dollars, we are at fifteen thousand, seven hundred, and fifty dollars for horses. Supplies, wagon, and team - four hundred thirty dollars, and pay for work before drive, ammunition, etcetera, two hundred eighty dollars. Let's see, that adds up to, uh, $16,460 before we make one cent." He chuckled, looked at the twins, "So far, so good. Let's meet the rest of the crew, shall we?"

The recruiting of drovers began with the first delivery from Maria de Castro who had three colored drovers among those that brought the horse herd to the Noche Buena. Eli spoke with all the drovers, but only the coloreds were interested. When he asked about their experience, he was impressed when Pete Staples said, "Wal, I rode with Bose Ikard on a cattle drive over the Goodnight Loving trail from Texas to Denver." Jim Perry explained, "I'se done worked on the XIT ranch, it's a litt'l place down Texas way," and John Swain shared, "I rode wit' John Slaughter's outfit, he were one o' dem Texas Rangers." Even though they all hailed from Texas, Eli said he wouldn't hold that against them and welcomed them to the bunkhouse on the Noche Buena.

He met up with Charlie Two Toes when he was on the El Toro rancho and they talked about the trail they would follow to the east and he said, "I've been over most of that trail many times. The Pony Express used much of that same trail, and I rode for the Express."

"Think you can scout for us, keep us on the trail and make good time?"

"I can do that."

He hired two vaqueros, Juan Bandini and Junipero Borremeo, from the drovers that delivered the horses for the Sargent brothers, another, Miguel Fages, was hired on by Jubal when they were at the Bolsa de Escarpines, where they failed to buy any horses, but at least found a drover. A pair of gauchos, Hipolito Bouchard and Pedro Portola, were both from Argentine families on the Santa Rita ranch where they were born, raised and learned their trade, and were anxious to see some new country, and although their families were not pleased with their leaving, they promised to return before the end of the year.

Eli was put onto the trail of Jeremy Webster and his wife, Missy, when he bought the wagon, team and harness from the owner of the El Alisal, the younger Bruno Bernal. "When we bought this wagon, Jeremy and his wife were going to go north with a cattle drive, but the drive did not go and that left Jeremy without work. We had nothing for a colored cook and his wife..." he shrugged. "Last I heard he was looking for work in Monterey. You might try the Café Lorraine, it ain't much but I think Jeremy was thinkin' he could get on there. Don't know 'bout his woman, though."

When Eli found Jeremy at the café and they talked, Jeremy asked, "Can I bring muh woman?"

"Is she your wife?" asked Eli.

"Yassuh, an' she helps me real good, cooks sometime too!" he grinned.

When Eli signed him on, Jeremy was happy as could be and when he found out he would be reunited with his cook wagon and the mule team, he was even happier.

———

JUBAL SUMMONED the drovers from the bunkhouse and the group gathered in front of the whitewashed adobe wall, most sitting on the low wall as everyone gathered around. Eli stood before them, looking from one to the other, "Men, I think we have a very good crew here and we need to work together from now to the end of the drive. We'll be pushing almost twelve hundred head over about thirteen hundred miles. It'll take us nigh unto three months, maybe longer. We'll be crossing a lot of dry land, maybe even hit some snow over the mountains, but I think we're timing it about right for the best weather and possible graze and water for the duration. You've met me and my sons," nodding to the twins, "and you've probably gotten acquainted with one another. Our cook, Jeremy," he pointed out Jeremy and his wife, "will have his wife as his helper so I 'spect all of you to be on your best behavior around the lady. Anything less will put you in jeopardy of missing out on some meals, compliments of the cook!" Everyone chuckled, most already knowing the necessity of treating the cook with the most respect because an upset cook could cause everyone to suffer in any number of ways from the taste of the food to the effect of the same.

"So, you'll take your orders from me or my sons, and I'm also going to have Mateo," nodding to the older caballero that had been the majordomo on the Rancho Noche Buena, "and Junipero, or Jun," one of the vaqueros, "as top hands to keep things in line. Charlie Two Toes will be our scout," nodding to the native Pawnee. "Also, you'll pick your horses each morning, and if you spot any that don't show they've been broke, and there are quite a few of those, I'll pay a dollar bonus for every one you break out."

He looked around, "Any questions?"

"When we leavin'?" asked John Swain.

"First light in the morning," responded Eli, "So get your rest tonight, it might be a while 'fore you get another good night's rest in a bunk."

CHAPTER 13

BEGINNING

Aruckus at the large corral brought Eli's attention back to the buildings and corrals. He had gone to the edge of the field on a slight rise that offered a view of the bay for his morning time with the Lord. He had enjoyed his solitude that began before first light, and the slow rising sun painted the sky behind him with shades of orange and pale pink that cast the colors on the incoming waves. But the snort of horses and the shouts of men brought him to his feet and started him walking back to the corrals.

A big strawberry roan had his head tucked between his front feet and was trying his best to kick the clouds from the sky as he twisted in the middle, took to the air and broke in half, but the rider dug his spurs into the ribs and held tight to the reins as he shouted, "Yeeeeehaahh!" Eli chuckled and picked up his pace, seeing most of the men gathered along the fence to watch the ride, while others were snubbing down another horse as Pete Staples grabbed the saddle horn and swung aboard, lead rope in hand. He stabbed his feet in the stirrups and nodded. One man jerked a rag from under the headstall that had covered the eyes of the big black, the other pulled back from his bear hug around the horses neck, and the black gelding exploded, bending in the middle as all four feet came off the ground. He twisted into a sunfish, bent his neck and head around trying to bite the leg of the rider, but the black man dug his big, roweled spurs into the ribs of the gelding and growled, "Is that the best you got blackie?"

A big bay horse and rider crow-hopped in the corner, but the gaucho Hipolito pulled the gelding's head down to his chest and leaned over the cantle of his saddle, letting the horse work out his protests. The strawberry roan had come to a spread-legged stop, his head down, his chest heaving, as he grunted and groaned, his jaw pulled tight by the steely grip of John Swain who sat like stone in the deep seated saddle, waiting for another explosion. The black with the diamond blaze on his forehead continued his kicking at the moon that still hung lazily in the western sky, and Pete Staples was grinning ear to ear and laughing all the while.

Two others, Juan Bandini and Junipero Borremeo were climbing aboard snubbed down horses, one a lineback dun, the other a steeldust grey, and they soon joined the melee, but their choices were not the early risers of the others and after a couple crow-hops, the two vaqueros nudged them to the fence to tether them down and finish rigging them out. Within the first half hour of dim light, all nine of the new hires had chosen their mounts from the strings they had brought in and were familiar with, but Jubal, Joshua and Eli preferred to ride their own mounts at least on this first day.

Eli walked to the big Concord wagon where Jeremy

and his wife, Missy, were finishing their packing and asked, "Anything you need, Jeremy?"

"No suh, reckon we gots ever'thin' we need, at least for the first stretch of this hyar jaunt." He leaned toward his woman, "What'chu think, Missy? We gots ever'thin'?"

"Ummmhmmm, nears I can tell," she answered as she was checking things off their list. They seemed to be a mis-matched pair, he was bigger than Eli, about a hand's width over six feet and easily topping out at well over two hundred pounds with a voice that came from the bottom of the well, but she was a wisp of a girl, less than five feet tall and skinny as a rail with a high pitched voice that sounded more like the squeak of a mouse, a little one at that.

Eli nodded, said, "We'll gather up o'er here by the fence, if you want to join us. I'll be lining out the overall plan of the trail."

"Yassuh, we be right thar, boss," answered Jeremy.

Eli shook his head, grinning, "Jeremy, you can call me Mr. McCain, Elijah McCain, or Eli. But we'll have none of that 'boss' stuff, alright?"

"Yassuh, that be fine boss, I means Eli, yassuh," he answered with a grin that split his black face with a mouth full of white teeth.

Eli chuckled, glanced at his woman and added, "That goes for you too, Missy."

"Yassuh," she answered, smiling with a sparkle in her eyes that bode a touch of mischief.

———

THE MEN GATHERED, but Eli noticed they all drew near those most familiar. The vaqueros were in their caballero attire that reminded Eli of his friend Candalario who was a *charro* and were dressed much the same with the short bolero jacket, big sombrero, tailored trousers and snug fitting chaps. Mateo was a vaquero, but his dress was less traditional and was more like the typical caballero or even the American buckeroo. The gauchos wore their traditional gear with the tall boots with bloused britches tucked in and held up by the decorated rastra, a flat hat with a narrow brim and chin strap called a chambergo and a panuelo or neck scarf, a loose jacket much like the bolero and a poncho draped over the cantle of their saddle. The three coloreds were attired like the typical caballero or what some were calling buckaroos, with the usual felt hat, linen shirt, canvas britches and high-topped boots all covered by the shotgun style chaps.

As the men squatted or stood by the fence, Eli looked them over and began. "Men, we'll be startin' out in a few moments, and we'll have prayer before we leave, but first I want to assign your places for today, and everything is subject to change as the need arises." He nodded to the Pawnee, "Charlie Two Toes and I will be scouting ahead, picking the trail and such, at least for today. We'll leave sign and we'll also do some hunting for meat for the camp. We'll be followed by our cook, Jeremy, in the wagon so they'll be the first to get to the next camp and start fixing the meals. Now, Junipero," pointing at the man standing in the middle of the three vaqueros, "and Pedro," the bigger of the two gauchos, "will start off on point. The first pair of swing riders will be Juan," a vaquero, "and Pete," the older colored. "The second pair of swing riders will be Miguel," a vaquero, "and Hipolito," the second gaucho. "They'll be ahead of the flank riders who will be Jim Perry and John Swain. Drag will be Jubal and Joshua. Each new day, everyone rotates back, today's drag riders will be tomorrow's point men and so on. Mateo and I will be moving back and forth, trying to help where we're needed. Any problems, come to me or Mateo or Jubal or Joshua. Any questions?" he asked, watching as the men looked at one another, but none spoke up.

Eli doffed his hat, said, "Let's have a quick prayer and we'll get started." As the men removed their hats and lowered their eyes, Eli began, "Our precious heavenly Father, we come to you in need today. We're starting a long journey and there will be plenty of challenges, but we know it will be nothing You cannot handle, so Lord, we're asking for your guidance, protection, and provision. We put our trust in you and ask that you keep your hands upon each of us. We ask these things in the name of our Lord and Saviour, Jesus Christ," he paused a moment, then closed with, "Amen!"

As he lifted his eyes and began to replace his hat, he noticed all the men doing the same and all had eager smiles on their faces as Eli said, "Drag and flank riders, circle behind 'em and start 'em movin'! Point men, open the gates and take your places!"

And the drive was on. The horses had been enjoying a lazy life on tall grass and fresh water, but now they milled about until two men pushed the leaders to the gate and when the others saw the leaders go through the gate, they were anxious to follow and the point men led the way, with the swing riders close behind and crowding the would be wanderers toward the leaders. Most herds have two swing riders, men that follow behind the leaders, always nudging the herd close behind and together, but with the long line of horses, there were two swing, two mid-swing, followed by two flankers, and with two drag riders bringing up the rear.

All the drovers knew the first few days would be the hardest with the more spirited horses wanting to break out on their own, although most would follow the herd, letting others lead the way. After several days on the trail, all the animals would know what was expected and needed, and most would move along as pushed. But this first day, all the riders were kept busy with the herd busters.

When Eli and Charlie Two Toes talked the night before as to the route of the drive, they agreed that if the first day would get them clear of some of the ranchos and into the open, it would make the drive easier. Charlie suggested, "If we make the Mission San Juan Bautista, they would probably allow us to stop for the night in one of their dormant fields. If we made it that far, we would have had a good day."

"Then that's what we shoot for, but if we still have daylight, we'll push on," said Eli, knowing that would become their mantra, 'if we still have daylight, keep movin'.

They started out to the north, soon bent a little to the northeast and by late morning were crossing the Salinas River, their first river crossing. But it went well, and the horses were still frisky and enjoying the stretch on the trail. They kept to the established roadways that usually marked the boundaries of the many ranchos until they came to the Diablo Range of hills and then Charlie chose to lead the drive on a stage road that split the hills and as he remembered, would take them to the Mission. The road that bordered the Natividad rancho brought them to the Gabilan creek and the stage road that would take them through the hills and to the mission.

When Jeremy caught up with the waiting Charlie and

Eli, he asked, "We noonin' today, or do we keep pushin'?"

"I reckon that's up to the cook. But for the first day, it wouldn't hurt to keep 'em movin'. Don't think they'd want to stop to eat and let 'em wander. Now, if'n you was to fix some biscuits and such we could take along…" answered Eli as he shrugged and grinned.

Jeremy grinned, "That's why I fixed us some extry biscuits. But I cain't wait an' feed 'em if'n I'm s'posed to be ahead o' the herd and stop fer supper."

"Then put 'em in a sack and I'll wait and hand 'em out. You and Charlie go 'head on."

Charlie said, "Hold on there, gimme a couple them and then we'll go 'head on."

Jeremy glanced to a grinning Eli, dug into the bag for a couple biscuits and handed them over the Charlie, then passed the bag to Eli. With a nod and a wave, the wagon and scout started to the hills, leaving Eli behind as he stepped down and led his claybank to the creek for a long drink.

CHAPTER 14

GABILAN

C harlie Two Toes was a good six to ten miles ahead of the herd, but when Eli thought he would have a bit of a break before the point men arrived, he was surprised to see Charlie coming back from the mouth of the valley in a long lope, looking about for any riders. Eli stood, waved Charlie near and as he reined up, Charlie was grinning as he explained, "I forgot to tell you, taking the herd through here there are three draws that branch off and we probably need someone at the head of each one to keep the horses on the right trail."

Eli looked back down the trail, saw the dust cloud that rode the heels of the herd, and said, "You take the furthest one, I'll get Mateo and he and I will take the first two. The drovers will have to wait till we get out the other side to get their food!"

"Will do!" answered Charlie as he spun his gelding around and took off back up the draw at a quick trot. Eli mounted up and swung Rusty around to ride back to find

Mateo, hopefully he would be near the point riders, if not, well, he would decide that when they came near.

He was pleased to see the herd lined out and coming at a good pace. They had already come about fifteen miles and the herd was bunched although stretched out. The roadways that were often sided by fencing or fencerows of trees, brush and rocks, kept the horses close, but when they hit the hills or the flats of the plains, they would space out. The draw before them had timber on the north and west facing slopes, while the opposing slopes were often covered with chaparral or bunch grass, but the steep slopes would make it easier for the drovers to push them through. As the herd neared, he spotted Mateo riding beside Junipero, one of the point men, and Eli stood in his stirrups and waved Mateo forward. Eli had thought of giving Mateo the title of majordomo since he was used to handling horses and men, but he would wait on that. As the man rode up and slid his mount to a stop, Eli said, "Side me!" and turned Rusty back to start up the long draw.

As they rode, Eli told Mateo, "There are three side draws that might be tempting for the horses to try so we'll need to block them off. You take the first one, I'll take the second, and Charlie will be waiting at the third. This is the Gabilan Range, but none of the hills are very big. Charlie says the draw will keep the horses close, so they should be easy to handle, long's we can keep them from taking a branch canyon."

Mateo looked at Eli, "I have been through here, made a trek to the San Juan Batista mission, but that was many years ago. It's not too far," he lifted his eyes to the sky and guessed the time to be early afternoon, "we should be out in less than an hour."

"Good. By the way," began Eli, as he dug in the bag, "here's some biscuits to keep you goin' till supper time."

"Gracias señor!" answered Mateo as he took the biscuits, wasting little time to bite into one. He nodded, pursed his lips, "These are good! I think you have a good cook for us!"

————

THE HERD MOVED EASILY into the wide mouth of the canyon that after about a half-mile made a dogleg bend to the east. Trees covered both the south and north facing slopes and the shoulders of the hills pushed toward one another. The thick timber was mostly oak, elm, and sycamore with a random ponderosa. But the long trunked trees allowed passage through the thick timber as they followed the stage road. At the apex of the bend, on the north edge of the canyon, the trees thinned and showed a cut between the knolls that sided the draw. When the point men and the leaders of the herd pushed their way through, the rest of the herd followed until they bunched up at the bend and one rank red dun gelding shouldered another horse aside, reared up and nickered and dropped into a run into the cut. Three other horses broke ranks and followed, right in front of the vaquero, Miguel Fages, who dug spurs in his mount and gave chase.

The escapees were running blind, but Miguel quickly read the lay of the land and took to the high side on the north, driving his mount through a small thicket, and broke out onto the bald shoulder. His movement turned the runaways to charge to the east over a low saddle and Miguel rode the high ground, forcing them to take the right-hand draw that pointed south, and he knew that would take them back to the herd. As the runaways crashed through the thick timber, they busted into the flank of the herd and Miguel followed, swinging wide of the herd to resume his place as the mid-swing rider. He shook his head at the restless runaways, but chuckled at how easily he and his mount handled them. He twisted around in his saddle, looking behind him and saw the flanker, Jim Swain with a broad smile as he stood in his stirrups to wave his hat in recognition of the successful chase. Miguel doffed his sombrero, waved back, and dropped into his saddle, pleased with the results of the chase, but he knew the day was not over and he kept a watchful eye on the herd.

The canyon widened to about two hundred yards and the herd spread out but were kept in check by the drovers. On the far side of the canyon from Miguel's return, Mateo sat on his mount, moving side to side, waving his sombrero and shouting, keeping the horses from escaping into the adjoining draw on the east side. Occasionally a horse would drop his head and try to cut by, but the well-trained mount of Mateo was quick and seldom let another horse near. His horse, a dapple grey mustang, would stretch out, teeth bared, and lunge at any attempt to get past, often nipping the outlaw mount back into the ranks of the herd.

When the herd passed the first fork, Mateo joined Jubal and Joshua at the drag, lifting his scarf over his mouth and nose to filter out the dust. Even though most of the canyon was grassy, with this many horses churning up the ground, some dust was inevitable. The men did not talk, just nodded, and kept at their work. Jubal and Joshua had quirts in hand and used them to wave off or encourage any stragglers. Too short to use as a whip, it was the movement and the accompanied shout that kept the animals in check.

Mateo moved alongside Jubal and suggested, "Perhaps you should get you a bullwhip or at least a buggy whip, señor."

"Never learned how to use 'em!" answered Jubal, having to shout to be heard over the thunder of hooves before them.

"I could teach you. It is not hard, and you could keep them in line easier." He patted the coil of braided leather that hung from his pommel. "I have found it helpful in many ways."

Less than a half mile further saw the second fork where Eli waited at the mouth of the draw. His big claybank stallion was not about to let any horses get past him and he fought any attempts with a nip and even shouldered two aside that almost went down but scrambled up and returned to the security of the herd.

Charlie waited another quarter mile on the east side and had less of a challenge with a narrow canyon that had thick timber on the south slope and nothing enticing to tempt any runaways, but he stayed busy waving them off. When it looked like most of the herd had passed and he saw the flanker John Swain, Charlie turned his mount and went up the draw to cross over the ridge and maybe get ahead of the herd.

At the head of the long and heavily timbered canyon, the stage road kept to the lower side of the north slope and climbed out of the canyon to cross over a saddle that blocked the way. The point rider, Pedro Portola, was forced to drop into the edge of the trees at the bottom of the saddle and drive the horses to the bald slope. The other point rider, Jun, stayed high on the slope and led the first of the leaders to cross over the end of the saddle. The herd streamed out behind the leaders and with Pedro driving, and Jun leading, they moved over the saddle, but once over, they were on a wider and bald hilltop that dropped off into the San Juan canyon below. The herd spread out, scattered across the hilltop and the first swing riders had to chase the many runaways into the trees and down the slopes into the canyon. The herd did not stampede, but it was a runaway as they dropped off the hillside and moved with the spread out herd, and the shouts, whistles and screams of the drovers echoed across the narrow draw.

The herd took the course of least resistance and headed north down the draw, seeing the grassy flats and smelling the water beyond. They did not stop until they reached the water of the San Benito River, where they congregated and splashed into the water, drinking their fill as the drovers surrounded them, but gave their own horses their heads and let them go into the water and drink as they wished.

The mouth of the canyon that was the place of escape for the herd, was just over a mile southeast of the Mission San Juan Batista, and fortunately, the trail followed by the horses did not cross any of the planted fields of the many resident Ohlone and Yokuts who had become a part of the mission family and were taught ranching and farming by the black robes. The mission also had many cattle, sheep, and horses and raised wheat, barley and corn. It was a fertile valley and had been well tended by the native residents.

When Eli sat watching the herd, Charlie came alongside and asked, "Would you want to talk to the fathers at the mission, see if they want to sell any of their horses?"

"Have you ever been here before?" asked Eli.

"Yes, many times. It is a good place. They always welcome visitors. I have stayed here before."

"Then you talk to them. I'll get the herd moving and we'll follow the river east, maybe find a place to make camp down there about where the river cuts through those hills. You can offer them fifteen dollars a head for as many as they want to sell, nothing over five years old and preferably broke to ride," explained Eli.

Charlie grinned, nodded, and started toward the mission that lay at the foot of the hills behind them, just west of the mouth of the canyon they had ridden through. Eli watched him go, motioned to Mateo and told him, "Let's get them moving before they start wandering. We'll follow the river," he pointed to the east, "Maybe make camp there at the cut."

CHAPTER 15

DIABLO

"The fathers at the mission said they have no horses to sell. He said the many Ohlone and Yokuts people that work the fields have need of all the horses they have," explained Charlie as he sipped at the hot coffee and reached for his plate of breakfast. He looked at Eli, "We go north now, take Pacheco Pass east, no?"

Eli chuckled, "Yes, we take Pacheco Pass east, but then we need to turn north. I'm thinking from what I could learn, we'll cross the San Joaquin valley and the river by the same name, then follow the Merced river east until we need to turn north. You're familiar with that route?"

"Eh," grinned Charlie, shaking his head and working on the mouth full of biscuit and sausage, "I've been over that way, it's as good as any, I reckon."

"How soon you think we'll get to the Sierra Nevada range?"

"A week, maybe a day or two sooner," answered Charlie, getting up to get more biscuits and gravy. He nodded to Jeremy when the cook filled his plate again, returned to his seat on the slab of rock, and asked Eli, "Think we'll hit snow in the Sierras?"

"Dunno. Everybody I talked to said this has been an open winter, so if we do, shouldn't be too much. Should be a good crossing."

Charlie grinned, "You been in the mountains much?"

"Not the Sierras, but been up and down the Rockies, Bitterroots, Cascades and more."

Charlie lifted his eyebrows and pursed his lips, "So, you ain't the tenderfoot I was thinkin', are you?"

Eli grinned, "The first time I was in the mountains, I'd reckon you were bouncin' on your momma's knee."

"Alright grampa, don't go showin' your age now. We might hafta put you in the back of a wagon!" chuckled Charlie.

Eli shook his head, grinned and stood, looked around the circle of men and glanced to the east to see the first edge of the rising sun as it colored the bellies of the clouds with a bright pink, "Hmmm, 'Red sky at mornin', sailors take warnin'. Hope that ain't true on this day!" declared Eli. He looked at the men, "Mount up! Let's get 'em movin'!"

———

THE HERD MOVED OUT and across the flats at an easy gait, the usual early morning fast step when all the animals were still a mite frisky and willing to try their escape from the herd. The drovers, especially the swing and flank riders, were kept busy, but managed well and with a change of mounts after they crossed Pacheco creek and took a break for nooning. The drive through the Diablo Range was much the same as the day before as the trail followed the long draw that was sided by steep slopes and heavy with timber. They pushed through the rolling hills and broke into the flats as they rode the north boundary of the Rancho San Luis Gonzaga, the rancho that was originally granted to Juan Carlos Pacheco, the namesake of the stagecoach road that crossed the Diablo Range and the creek that marked the way for the road.

The sun was making long shadows of the hills when Eli gave the signal to gather the herd and make camp for the night. Jeremy and Missy had been busy preparing the supper for the men and as the herd was settled and some of the riders came to the camp, the drovers appreciated the efforts of the two. As Missy filled the plates, Jeremy told Eli, "We'll be needin' some fresh meat 'fore too long. We gots 'nuff fer mebbe two, three meals."

"How you fixed on everything else?" asked Eli, accepting the full plate from Missy.

"We fine on the rest, gots plenty flour, sugar, corn-meal an' such, it's just meat we need."

Eli looked at Charlie who had been the first through the line, "Hear that Charlie?"

"Yup," was the only answer offered by the scout who was busy cleaning his plate and hoping for more before the rest of the crew came in to the fire. He looked up as Eli sat nearby and said, "Should be able to get a deer or two when we cross the San Joaquin River and follow the Merced."

"I might ride up there with you, double our chances with two of us huntin'," suggested Eli.

"Sounds good to me. That way I can be further out ahead an' you can take the meat to the cook."

Eli glanced at Charlie and knew the scout was not shirking his duty but preferred to be at least a half-day ahead of the herd for his scouting. Eli had already formed his opinion of the scout and was confident in his work, comfortable that Charlie knew the land and could scout the trail for any hazards or dangers for the herd. If he was scouting for a wagon train, the river crossings, roadways, trails and hazards, would be considerably different than for a herd of over a thousand horses.

Continuing northeast, they moved across the flatlands, bypassing the farms and ranchos, staying near the south bank of the Merced river and spent the night with the herd kept on a bit of a peninsula where the river bent back on itself. With a neck of about a half mile and the rest of the isthmus bordered by the river and the thickets that lined the bank, the men had an easy night keeping the herd together. With another early morning start, they followed the Merced a short distance, crossed over without mishap and turned north. Charlie told Eli they should come to the Tuolumne River when they saw the lawless settlement of LaGrange.

Eli asked, "Lawless?"

Charlie chuckled, "Yup, they ain't never had a lawman of any kind and it's been there since 'fore the '49 rush. Still got some doin' some gold diggin', pannin' an' such. Even got 'em a school, but they ain't got no law. But from what I hear, you don't want to go upsettin' folks cuz they take care of their own. Got 'em a hangin' tree right by the river." He laughed, "So, I ain't goin' near that town. But there is a purty good tradin' post if Jeremy needs anything."

Eli shook his head, grinning, "I'll keep that in mind."

"Nother day north we'll come to Sonora an' they got a good store too," offered Charlie before reining his mount around and starting off at a trot with a wave over his shoulder to Eli.

They crossed the Tuolumne downriver from LaGrange, made an easy crossing and pointed the herd northeast. Charlie said to keep to the long plateau, "There's some deep canyons on the upper end of the Tuolumne, but if you keep to the flats you'll come to a place where there's a long ridge running east/west and 'nother'n off your right that runs north/south. That'll make a purty good place to hold the herd an' get some sleep, if'n your of a mind. Then you'll turn east into the hills an' 'bout everwhere you look, there's signs o' gold diggin'. But there's a road there that'll take you on to Sonora. I'll be meetin' up with you 'fore you get there."

The herd was stretched out for about a half-mile, a long thin line of horses moving three and four abreast as they followed the wagon road that had been well-used by the many '49ers, but it had never been used for anything but freight wagons and miners wagons. With a thousand head of horses moving along the dusty road, they were dragging a good-sized dust cloud and as the herd neared the settlement of Sonora, many of the townsfolk and miners from the diggings had come near the road to see the unusual sight. When Eli and the point men passed by, some shouted out, "Whar' ya' goin' wit' so many nags?"

"East, they're for the army that's fightin' the Indian wars!" declared Eli.

And the chatter started among the settlers, being totally unaware of any Indian wars, they were immediately worried that they might be attacked by natives at any moment, not knowing the Indian wars were over a thousand miles away. Eli just shook his head and chuckled and kept the herd moving. Jeremy had gone before them to resupply at the general store and had been seen moving out ahead of the herd. He kicked up the mules to a trot and left his own cloud of dust for the point men to cough and spit, but he planned on a good supper for them all that would make them forget about any road dust.

The men were surprised when they rode into camp to find a row of fresh baked apple pies waiting. They walked near, sniffed the air but the pies were under the watchful eye of Missy who stood close by with a meat cleaver in her hand and one eyebrow cocked up and eyes squinted that dared any man to try for the pie. But none dared to lose any fingers and

went for their supper to enjoy the corn meal biscuits, fresh venison provided by Charlie, mixed vegetables bought from a roadside farmer, and potatoes and gravy. But everyone saved room for some apple pie.

CHAPTER 16

SIERRA NEVADA

"Why didn't you tell me this was a toll road?" asked Eli, talking to Charlie as they mounted up to resume their trek.

"Sorry boss, but the last time I was through here was a few years back and it wasn't a toll road then. But after what that man said, it should be easier goin' for the herd," answered Charlie.

"Easier goin'? He wasn't even sure if we could make it! But at least he didn't charge us anything. I think he was hopeful we would make it cuz that'd open the road and folks would start using it sooner. But we'll hafta leave the herd behind somewhere and you and I will ride ahead, see what we find."

"That feller back there said the best place to make a stop would be at Long Barn an' if I remember right, there is a nice basin just past the buildin's."

"How much further?" asked Eli.

Charlie looked at the sun, "Oh, we'll make it 'fore sundown."

With woolen union suits, chaps over their trousers,

coats and extra blankets in their bedrolls, the intrepid group of explorers set out to scout the road to Sonora Pass. Led by Eli and Charlie, the others in the group, all packing shovels, were Joshua, Jubal, and the two gauchos, Hipolito and Pedro, who had volunteered for the trek. The two gauchos were snug in their wool ponchos and grinned at the others as they started out in the dim cold light of early morning.

By mid-day they came to the end of the road that straddled the long ridge and the road bent down into a creek bottom to cross over to another ridge. Atop the ridge, the wind had kept the winter's snowfall clear except for patches in the shelter of thick trees, but the road had been clear. Now as it dropped into the creek-bottom, white showed among the trees and what had been a creek, was a long sliver of ice that lay under the drifted snow. Eli reined up at the edge of the trees still atop the ridge, the grey packhorse came alongside, glad to be with his buddy, Rusty. Eli stood in his stirrups for a better look and dropped into his saddle and turned to look at the others. "Well fellas, this is where our work begins. I'll lead off, the snow is nothing new for Rusty here," as he leaned down to stroke the stallion's neck, "and we'll buck the small drifts, but I'm thinkin' we'll need to do some shovelin' down in the bottom."

And shovel they did. At places, the drift with its thin crust of ice was five and six feet deep, but once the crust was broken, the snow was grainy and easily shoveled. They could hear the chuckle of water underneath the thick ice and when the snow was clear, the ice was thick and would probably break with the weight of the wagon, but it was no more than four feet across at its widest and the water would be shallow. When it was clear enough for a couple horses to pass, Eli and Charlie left the others to widen the trail and scatter dirt and branches across the ice of the little creek and make it safer to cross for both horses and the cook wagon. As Eli mounted, he looked at Jubal, "You're in charge, Jubal. I'm takin' the grey with us and Charlie and I will go a bit further, find some place to stop for our next camp, maybe break some trail. But we will keep going. As soon as you're done here, go on back to camp, get everything ready to move out early in the morning. We'll either be waiting for you up yonder a ways, or we'll leave sign for your next camp."

"Got it, Pa. We'll get it done," declared Jubal with a glance to Joshua. Eli was trusting his sons to accept the mantle of responsibility and he could not help but think about his purpose for this entire drive. It had little to do with the money they expected to make, but everything to do with helping the twins become the men he hoped. After their history of running away, quitting jobs, and shirking responsibility, he hoped this drive and the possible future of married life would help them to mature and become the men he believed them to be and fulfill their mother's dream.

When they came up from the draw, the road angled across the face of the timbered slope and cut back on itself as it crested the ridge. The road continued to meander, taking the path of least resistance through the timber and rolling hills. When the road bent around a bit of a knoll, Charlie reined up and waited for Eli to come alongside. "We shouldn't have much trouble keepin' the horses on the road, this timber's thick and dark. But if you look yonder," he pointed off to their left or west, "that there's the Middle Fork of the Stanislaus River and that canyon's 'bout two thousand feet deep. Don't wanna have any them horses traipsin' too close to that."

"Don't reckon," replied Eli. "Must be a mite cold down there. You'd think we could hear the roar of the river, less'n there's too much ice."

"I ain't gonna look. Don't like heights!" declared Charlie, nudging his mount back to the road.

A common sight on both sides of the road, mostly where there was a creek, there were prospect holes, broken sluices and other debris and evidence of gold hunters. When the rush was on in '49 and after, the hills were crawling with prospectors, most of whom had no idea what they were doing but all were looking for something shiny and the color of gold and they left traces of where they had been all over the hillsides and valleys.

Where the trees were thick, white showed on the ground, some were drifts, others just the winter accumulation. But if the sun had pierced the pine canopy, the ground was damp with melted snow but showed only the fallen needles of the sugar pine, redwoods, ponderosa and more. When the trail took a bend to the east to follow the contour of the land, they came onto an old burn that left the pilloried pines and their skeletal remains, now grey with age but black clinging to the bottom of the once majestic trunks. The hillsides looked like an army of long dead scarecrows standing at attention across the face of all the nearby hills. At the base of the slope, the road twisted through nature's cemetery and showed a bit of a basin that caught Eli's attention. "That'd be a good place to hold the herd for a night," as he stood in his stirrups and pointed with his chin. It was the confluence of three valleys, one carrying a small creek and patches of snow, but little white showed for the sun had done its job in dispelling winter's wrath.

A glance to the sun and Eli guessed there to be two to

three hours of daylight left. He looked at Charlie, "Wanna go further, see what's down yonder?"

"Down there's where the old road follows the Clark Fork, but the toll-taker said the new road bends down through Dead Man's Creek. That'll be 'nother three, four miles, an' you won't like the look of it."

Eli shook his head, "Why?"

"The trail sides a steep mountain, kind of an eyebrow trail, if'n you know what I mean."

"I know what an eyebrow trail is, but that fella said this road was worked over and is a good wagon road. If that's the way it is, it might be alright. But now that you said that, we need to look." He twisted around in his saddle and with another look at the sun, glanced to Charlie, "Lead on scout!"

When the trail made a dog leg bend to the west, it was headed to the rim of the canyon. Eli frowned and asked, "How close does this get to the edge of the cliffs?"

"Dunno now, it's been a while. . ." but he was stopped when his horse shied, nickered as he side-stepped and looked to the trees on the right.

Rusty twitched, his ears pricked, and he looked to the trees with nostrils flaring, the grey sided the claybank, both nervous and skittish, and Eli felt the nicker come from deep in Rusty's chest. Both men held a tight rein, and Eli snatched at his rifle in the scabbard under his right leg. He slipped it out, jacked a round into the chamber and asked, "See anything?'

"No, but there's somethin' they don't like," declared Charlie, leaning forward and looking into the deep woods that climbed the rocky bluff to the right of the road.

Eli took a deep breath, "Can't be a bear, don't smell

anything and the wind's in our faces. It's a little early for them to be comin' out of hibernation."

"Bears do what bears wanna do, nobody tells 'em different," declared Charlie, reaching down to stroke the neck of his mount, talking to him to settle him down. He glanced to Eli's stallion, "I think the horses are settlin' down a mite."

"Whatever it was, they didn't like. Coulda been wolves, cougar, bear, maybe even coyotes."

Charlie nudged his mount to the road, and he stepped out. Rusty followed and Eli lay his rifle across the pommel. Charlie nodded to Eli, "We've got to come back this way, less'n you wanna make camp further down."

"Let's keep goin' and might find something else. But whatever that was, I'd like to run it off or get rid of it. We don't need the herd stampeding anywhere around here."

CHAPTER 17

NARROWS

"Ah, this ain't too bad," declared Eli. "I've been on eyebrow trails that were so narrow I had to take my foot out of the inside stirrup and the outside stirrup was hanging over the edge. This is a good wagon road and if there's room for wagons and teams, there's room for a horse herd." He looked at the outside edge, and through a break in the trees could see the steep drop-off, "Whadda'ya reckon, 'bout a thousand feet down there to the bottom?"

Charlie chuckled, "Whatever it is, I don' wanna find out, personal, that is. But there's lotsa trees to stop you if you step off."

"In some places," answered Eli, craning to look over the edge.

The shelf road started around a big round shoulder that jutted out into the canyon and the steepest drop-off was at the point of the bend. Towering sugar pines, Douglas fir, ponderosa and more crowded the edge and stood like protective pillars lining the roadway. Wherever the timber was heavy, patches of drifted snow stretched across the road, but nothing too deep for Rusty to break trail. The trees, some towering over two hundred feet, gave a false sense of security but both Eli and Charlie knew the danger of stepping too close to the loose dirt at the far edge. The near side showed sign of blasting where the road builders had to drill and blast through massive rock faces and sheer cliffs to cut the road through, yet even though the roadbuilders finished their work two to three years prior, already there were seedlings taking root in the narrow crevices and rocky faces.

The road dipped into a notch and back out to round another knob before breaking into the open on a face of a gentler slope with thinning trees. They stopped on the crest of a hill with another stand of dead trees that told of a more recent fire, but through the cadaverous stand, Charlie pointed, "There's the Clark Fork and that's where the road used to be, but this new toll road takes us on the middle fork of the Stanislaus River and into Dead Man Creek. From here, it's about a day 'fore we turn north on the Walker, then another two, probably three days north to Fort Churchill."

"Think we'll run into any snow worse'n what we've seen?"

"Don't think so. There'll prob'ly be some places we might hafta shovel, but…" he shrugged.

Eli glanced to the sky, "We've got time, let's go back to the place where we'll have the herd make camp and make our own camp. I'm gettin' hungry!"

————

THE RISING sun threw lances of gold that illumined the tall rimrock mesa to the south of the camp and Eli, having already had his alone time with his Lord, sat by the fire sipping his coffee as the rest of the crew rolled from their blankets. Jeremy and Missy had readied their breakfast and the men willingly filled themselves on the johnny cake, strip steaks, and hot coffee. Eli gathered the men around and began, "Today's drive is gonna be a bit of a challenge. This road goes through that cut behind me, then rounds a point and hangs over the canyon of the Middle Fork of the Stanislaus River. It's a good road, mostly wide and flat with trees on both sides, but the outside edge is soft and it's about a thousand feet to the bottom. So, don't go rushing or crowdin' the horses, let 'em take it at their own pace and we'll make it alright. One more thing, our horses got spooked yesterday by somethin', bear or cougar or somethin', and it's probably long gone. But Charlie, Mateo, and I will space ourselves out along that road on the uphill side where any predator might be waiting and if there is one, we'll do our best to scare it away or kill it on sight. So, if you hear some shootin'…" he shrugged. Looking around at the men, he saw only eagerness in their eyes and nodded, "Then let's get movin'!"

With a nod to Charlie and Mateo, and a wave to Jeremy to head out with the cook wagon, Eli went to his horses, both were saddled and rigged and ready, but he slipped the Spencer from the pack, thinking he might need the bigger rifle today. He slipped it into the spare scabbard that hung under his left leg and mounted up. Eli led the way and stationed Mateo at the point of the first wide bend where the hills were almost solid rock, but still held scattered trees. This was the only point where a predator could come from either side. Charlie took a point on the wide bend that hung over the canyon, but with thick timber, a wily predator could choose that place for an attack. Eli intentionally took the stretch he thought would be the most likely and was near where the horses had spooked the previous day. It was after the road rounded the last big point and dipped into a notch that also had a small runoff creek, before bending around the last lesser point and entering the burn area. He thought the presence of water, even though not much more than a trickle, would be the difference.

At the notch, he pointed Rusty into the trees, moved to a slight shoulder and stepped down. The shoulder was away from the creek and offered three different escape routes. He ground tied the big horse, spoke to both of them, "Now, you two keep a good watch. I'm gonna be on that escarpment yonder and I can see you and you can see me, so if there's somethin' you don't like, warn me. Got that?" he asked, knowing if anyone heard him they would probably think him daft, but he had a special understanding with his horses, as do most western men.

As the trees crowded in and narrowed the roadway, the herd stretched out almost three quarters of a mile. Moving mostly three abreast, they stepped out at a good pace and were led by the two point men, Jubal and Joshua, it was their second time on point. Along the line, the swing riders and flankers stayed on the outside, and were spaced out accordingly. The timber and steep hill-sides kept the uphill side of the herd in place. It was a pleasant morning, the air was cool, and the breeze rose from the canyon, sweeping up the steep hillsides and whispering through the branches. The men had no need of shouting, cracking of whips, or any of the usual moves necessary to keep the horses moving, they seemed to sense the purpose of the day and steadily kept the pace.

Yet even on the cool morning and with thick timber siding the road, the big herd stirred up the dusty road and dragged a cloud of dust on their tail, forcing the drag riders to lift the scarves over their faces. When the herd passed the first big bend, Mateo fell in with the drag riders, Junipero and Pedro. The herd moved steadily and was watched by Charlie as they passed his point, but he also was vigilant of the entire area, especially the uphill side. The trees afforded cover for any predator, and he was standing, rifle held across his chest as he searched the shadows and the breaks of the trees but saw nothing. As the herd moved past, the dust began to obscure his vision, but still he searched. Nothing. When he heard the approach of the drag riders, he swung back aboard his mount and dropped through the trees to join them.

Then the world seemed to explode! Horses were wheeling around, nickered, snorting, shoving against one another, charging directly at the drag riders and the men were forced to turn and put their horses into a gallop to escape the charging herd. The four men were laying low on the necks of their mounts, the thundering herd close behind, all with heads stretched out and eyes wide, manes flying, tails erect as they fled whatever had spooked them.

Eli watched as the lumbering herd approached, he knew the cook wagon had already passed, and saw the twins on point, but knew they could not see him. They were riding side by side, talking, but attentive to the herd behind them, always twisting around in their saddles to look. They passed Eli's promontory and the first eight or ten horses had passed, when the entire herd seemed to move to the side and a big brown monster crashed from the trees. The roar of the charging grizzly rumbled across the canyon and echoed back as the beast barreled into the nearest horse, a frightened buckskin mare that started to rear, eyes wide and mouth open, but the big bruin buried his teeth in the exposed neck and dragged the mare to the ground.

The smell of the beast, the roar of the charge, the presence of the monster startled all the horses that screamed, reared up and pawed at the sky, bucked and tried to kick at the brown monster. The bear, front paws on the chest of the dead and bleeding buckskin, cocked his head to the side and with fangs showing he growled a roar that shook the trees, and Eli's Spencer barked, bucked and spat fire and lead. The bullet struck the bear on the front shoulder, Eli saw the dust rise, but the bear swatted at the nuisance, and roared his challenge again.

All the nearby horses had stampeded and the thunder of a thousand horses running reverberated throughout the canyon. Again the Spencer barked, fire and smoke piercing the trees before Eli, but he had a clear shot and the bullet struck again. But still the beast pawed at the air with one paw, roared his complaint again, and Eli jacked another .52 caliber bullet into the chamber, cocked the hammer and let the lead fly again. This bullet took the beast lower on his chest, and Eli thought he could see blood on the brown fur, but he jacked another round and fired again and again and again. He knew each bullet pierced the fur, but the beast was still atop the downed horse and ripping at the flesh with his long claws, grabbing at the exposed meat with his bloodied teeth, and lifted his head, meat hanging from his mouth, as he turned to face Eli.

Eli had moved a little closer, and now was on one knee on the point of the promontory that overlooked the road. He was no more than forty yards from the beast, and he took aim again. The monster was glaring directly at Eli as he cocked his head to the side and opened his jaws wide and let another roar come from deep within.

Eli sent his bullet into the mouth of the beast to explode out the back of his head and finally the monster dropped to the ground, stretched out beside the carcass of the buckskin mare.

When the horses shied away from the charging grizzly, they crowded against one another and pushing and shoving and screaming and stumbling, several horses were pushed off the precipice at the edge of the road. One of those horses was the favorite gelding ridden by Hipolito and the herd pushed against any resistance and the horses gave way as the others were pushed off the road. But the hillside was steep and crowded with towering sugar pine and Douglas fir, yet that proved to be a bit of an advantage. The big trees overshadowed any undergrowth and the proven horseman, the gaucho Hipolito, drove his feet deep in the stirrups, leaned far back over the cantle of his saddle and keeping a taut rein, did his best to help his horse stay upright. The hillside was so steep, the rider felt the rump of the horse with his shoulders, could not see the head of his horse past the flying mane, and the animal drove his front hooves into the pine needles, broken branches, and moist soil to slow his descent, his back hooves and legs digging deep as he slid on his rump through the churned soil and pine needles.

Hipolito took ragged breaths, ducking and twisting as pine boughs slapped at him and tried to drive into his body, his iron grip on the reins unrelenting and his legs stiff as his feet were deep into the tapaderos. He thought he heard the screams and more from other horses that had been shouldered off the road and into the trees, but he saw nothing but trees and more trees. Suddenly the horse drove his front feet deep, lunged up, and drove them down again, and came to a stop, shaking and trembling, head hanging and drawing a ragged breath. Hipolito jumped to the ground, went to the head of the horse and hugged the animal, talking all the while and thanking and soothing the animal. When they both had their breath, Hipolito looked around and shook his head, wondering how he was going to get out of these trees and back up that steep hillside. But a quick look over the edge of the bluff to the river below, and he dropped to his knees, made the sign of the cross over his chest, and began giving thanks to the Lord.

CHAPTER 18

DEAD MAN

The round-up started immediately. After settling the few horses that were in the lead with Jeremy and Missy in a little basin at the confluence of the Clark Fork and the Middle Fork of the Stanislaus Rivers, the twins returned to help Eli dispose of the carcass of the bear and the dead horses. Besides the one killed by the grizzly, two others with broken legs had to be put down.

The shots of the put downs reverberated across the canyon, but a short delay later, Eli heard the report of a pistol that came from below. He looked at the twins, "That might be one of our men, might'a gone downhill after some horses and may need some help."

"I'll go Pa," offered Jubal.

Eli looked at his son, slowly nodded, "Best do it on foot. Ain't no place 'tween here'n last night's camp that's fit for horse, not on the downhill side anyway."

"Maybe I should go with him, Pa," suggested Joshua.

"Both of ya' go, that way you can help each other. That's a mighty steep slope so look it over real good before you start." He looked from one to the other, "I'll do back that way, see if I can help the others with the round-up. I reckon those horses are scattered all over these mountains. If you find anybody down there and need some help, fire off three rounds and either I'll come, or somebody else will." He looked about, went to his horse and took the rawhide reata he always had and handed it to Joshua, "And if you can find any other, you might be better off with as much as you can carry." He held on to the riata a moment, then motioned with his finger for Jubal to follow and he went to the packs on the grey, dug around a bit and handed him a hand axe and a shovel. "Don't take any unnecessary chances, hear me?"

"We hear ya, Pa," answered Jubal.

Eli nodded, stepped aboard his claybank and with the grey following close behind, started back down the road, searching the ground and the trees for tracks or sign of any wayward horses. When he rounded the big shoulder, he saw movement at the edge of the trees and nudged Rusty nearer. Crawling up to the road, John Swain was struggling, groaning, and if Eli heard right, the black man was praying. Eli stepped down, called out, "John? Hold on there, I'll come down and give you some help."

"Praise be, I done thought weren't gonna be nobody to find me! Mistuh Eli, you be careful, that there dirt's mighty loose. I done slid back here twict!"

Eli cautiously side-stepped, digging in his heels and grabbed onto a long branch of a close at hand ponderosa, and moved close to the belly-down John. "You got a broke leg or what?"

"I think it's broke, an' I twisted th' other ankle som'pin awful," he gasped for breath, "An I think I got me some broke ribs. I'se a mess aw'right, might hafta just shoot me like some ol' bronc wit' a broke leg!" he started to chuckle, winced at the pain and grabbed his side.

It took a while to get John up on the road, get his leg splinted, and bandages and wraps on his other wounds and Eli stood back and with hands on hips, frowned and shook his head, "Maybe you were right. If I'da just shot you, it woulda been a sight easier!"

John grinned, gasped, "Oh, that hurts," as he grabbed as his side. "Don't go funnin' me. It hurts too much to laugh!"

Eli grinned, "What makes you think I was funnin' you?"

It was a struggle to get John aboard Rusty, and Eli said, "Think you'd ride easier if you had me in the saddle to hold on to, or will you be better alone?"

"If'n we can," he struggled to sit up straight to make breathing easier, "it'd be easier to have somethin' to hold onto."

They started back to the basin and as they came to the sight of the grizzly attack, Eli was surprised to see Joshua climbing up from below. "Hey Pa! We found Hipolito down yonder, there were three horses with him, all a little scratched up, he had to put one down and another'n broke his neck. He said he thought one or two went over the edge and ended up in the river below. He and Jubal are taking the three and Hipo's horse out through the trees and I come to get our horses."

"Hipo alright?" asked Eli.

"Eh, scratched up a little, but other'n that, he's alright."

"Then come on, I'm taking John here to the wagon, and then we can go together back down the road and help the others with the round-up."

"Hipo, you get Missy to tend to your cuts and scrapes

and when you're ready, get a fresh horse and come on down with the rest of us. We," he motioned to Jubal and Joshua, "will go ahead and help the others," but the sound of horses coming from the road above them stopped him and Eli shaded his eyes against the lowering sun and looked to the tree lined road. Horses came thundering down the cut-off road that had been the old wagon road toward the basin where the cook wagon had been set-up and the few horses were gathered.

Eli grinned, stood with the reins of his claybank in hand and watched as horses came down into the basin. The leaders of the herd splashed across the shallow waters and joined the others who stood with heads high, and ears pricked. It was like a family reunion as the horses milled about, sniffing and nuzzling one another, but it did not take long for Eli to see this was less than half the herd. As the three riders that followed them pushed the rest across the shallow Middle Fork and into the basin with the Clark Fork, Eli watched as they settled the gather, and one rider came near. It was Charlie Two Toes who reined up, grinning, and leaned on the pommel of his saddle. "Supper ready?" he asked.

Eli grinned and chuckled, "Not my job, but I think Jeremy and Missy are gettin' the job done. What's the word?"

Charlie sat up, pushed his hat back on his head and explained, "Mateo said the rest of 'em will camp back there where we did last night. It'll take another day to get the runaways and stragglers, but we thought it'd be best to get these up here. We did leave some so the others'd know they hadn't been left. Mateo figgers, and I agree, that if there's a bit of a herd there, some o' the others'll come outta the trees on their own. But he did say if some of us wanna come back in the mornin' and help, he would not object." He grinned and leaned on his elbows on the pommel.

Eli nodded, "Anybody hurt?"

"Nah, scared a mite cuz it was a race to the woods, that's for sure. Thot we might take a dip in the river down below a time or two, but we made it alright."

"We had one man pushed over the edge, he's beat up some, broke leg and more. John Swain. And Hipo took a ride through the trees, said we lost some down there, couple went in the drink, couple more had to be put down."

Eli looked up at Charlie, "Me'n the boys will watch 'em, you and those two," nodding to Jim Perry and Miguel Fages, "strip your horses and let 'em out, get ready for supper. After you eat an' rest up, then you can watch 'em while we eat. Did you get a count?"

"More of a guess, mebbe five hundred."

"Sounds like we've got some work to do."

"Yup."

———

BY THE END of the very long day, a tired bunch of riders pushed the rest of the herd into the basin. By their best count, they had only lost about twenty-five horses. There were a few that were limping and would need attention with minor cuts and scrapes, but the horses were tired, and none appeared skittish or fearful. When the riders, except for the night riders, dragged into camp for supper, Mateo looked at Eli, "We moving out at first light?"

Eli grinned, shook his head, "If any of us are awake, yeah."

Mateo chuckled, turned to his bedroll and was soon

sound asleep and joined the symphony of snores, snorts, moans, and groans, and more as the tired crew slipped into a deep sleep.

Jeremy and Missy had prepared a veritable feast for the well-deserving riders, and nothing is more pleasant to wake up to than the smell of fresh-baked biscuits, bacon grilling, potatoes frying, and gravy bubbling. Of course the smell of percolating coffee helps too. It was a smiling crew that rolled out of their blankets and the fresh, cool, mountain air filled their lungs, the orange tint in the eastern sky was making the darkness retreat, and laughter filled the camp. Even though they knew their route would be along Dead Man Creek, it was a good day to be alive and every man there knew it and was thankful.

CHAPTER 19

CANYON

The first part of the trail pushed into the canyon of the West Fork of the Stanislaus River and sided the river for about six or seven miles. The shoulders of the hills pushed in and showed steep and often bald slopes that kept the horses on the road. After the previous stampede and roundup, the horses had become a little more meek-minded and were somewhat complacent and willing to keep to the roadway. After the road bent around an isolated rocky knob, it started to climb the east wall of the canyon to cross over a massive rock outcrop that had a long talus slope dropping into the canyon bottom.

Once around the promontory, the trail took to the canyon of the Deadman Creek, making a switchback to climb higher on the slope to take to a slight shoulder and move deeper into the canyon. The road was similar to that of the previous days travel with hillsides thick with towering sugar pine, ponderosa, and a scattering of redwood. Thick chapparal with manzanita, scrub oak, and various berry bushes filled in the gaps to paint the entire slopes on both sides of the canyon in varying shades of greens.

"Here they come," declared Charlie, glancing to Eli.

"They're moving right along. I think the horses have become used to the trail and following the point men and leaders," observed Eli, turning back around in his saddle, "Let's keep moving, looks like we're getting into a narrower canyon."

"Yeah, once in there, there's no place for them to go but on the road."

Rising steeply on both sides of the roadway, shear precipices of solid rock stood tall reminding Eli of ancient ogres looming over the miniscule figures on the snake-like road that twisted through the narrow canyon. As the two men rode into the canyon, the only sound was the clatter of their horses' hooves on the hard-packed wagon road. Yet even that sound reverberated through the rocky narrow canyon. Eli noticed the absence of any other sound, no chipmunks chattered, no marmots whistled, and no songs trilled from any birds. Eli scanned the treetops, the sky, and their surroundings, but saw no sign of life and the canyon seemed eerily silent. Even the chuckle of the small stream below had the trickle and splashing muted by the close-in shrubbery and willows.

The canyon of Dead Man Creek was only about a mile and a quarter long, with the last quarter mile opening a little, and the steep walls on the south face showed the lower half as wide grey talus slopes fell from the overhanging dark grey stone face. The roadway ricocheted off the gray stone to turn north into a long but wider valley that carried an almost dry runoff creek bed of no-name creek. The valley bottom was heavy with chapparal, sage, and bunch grass. Most of the trees were thickets of lodgepole pine, and the road was clear and easy-going. The drovers moved off the road, allowed the horses to range about a bit and snatch mouthfuls of grass, but kept them moving at a steady pace.

The wider valley carried them about two miles north before bending to the east for another four miles and turned back to the north along Leavitt Creek. Charlie and Eli rode beside one another as Charlie glanced to the sun, "I reckon it's nigh unto another six, eight miles until the road breaks into a nice wide meadow that'd make a good camp for the night. Good water, grass, and such, if'n you're wantin' to quit a mite early."

Eli also glanced to the sun, held out his hand to measure the distance between the sun and the horizon, pursed his lips, "Six, eight miles?"

"'Bout."

"We got a couple hours of daylight, but if it's a good grassy place, good water, maybe it'll do 'em good to have a bit of a break, so, yeah, that'll do," answered Eli. He looked at Charlie, "You go ahead, I'll drop back and tell Jeremy so he can get the cook wagon set up, and I'll catch up with you."

Charlie nodded, kicked his mount up to a trot and Eli moved aside to wait for Jeremy and his wagon to come alongside. As the wagon neared, Jeremy nodded, "Howdy boss! Uh, I mean, Eli. Got us a spot to make a camp yet?"

"'Bout another six, eight miles further up. Charlie said it drops off into a nice grassy valley with good water, so…" he shrugged and grinned.

"Say, Eli, if'n it's a good place, an' seein' how

tomorrow is Sunday, what say we have us a church service?"

"A church service?"

"Yassuh, I been noticin' you have yo' time wit' da' Lord, so I thot mebbe you'd like us to have church."

"You a preacher are you?" asked Eli, grinning.

"I is. I preached the Word lotsa times. Any time I can speak fo' da' Lord, I'se happy to do it!"

Eli chuckled, "Then we'll just hafta to do that, but it'll be at first light!"

"Tha's the way I like's it!" He pointed to the eastern horizon, "Gettin' up wit' da' sun fo' da' Son!" and pointed to the heavens, "Yassuh!"

————

JEREMY STOOD before the men who were gathered in the shade of some cottonwoods and whispering ponderosa at river's edge. He sported a broad grin that showed white teeth against his dark skin, sparkling eyes that promised everything, as he began, "Fellas, I ain't no preacher, I'se just a cook, but I'se a man what loves Jesus! Yassuh! And what we been through in the past few days got me ta' thinkin' 'bout Heab'n and the hopes that ever'body has 'bout goin' thar. But ain't ever'body what knows what it takes ta' git thar.

"Now, if'n I was to ax all you'ns what you thot you had to do to git ta' Heab'n, I reckon some o' you'sed say, 'Got's to work hard at it, be good man, an' such.' Then some'd say, 'Got to go ta' church, do all them things what the preacher says,' but all dose things ain't in the good Book." He held up his mother's old, tattered Bible, pointed at it with his free hand and continued. "My momma showed me when I was barefoot an' in knee britches, where an' what it say. And she say, 'God wouldn't tell us 'bout Heab'n wit'out showin' us an' tellin' us how ta' git thar. And He wouldn't make it hard, cuz God loves us all, ever' one o' us just the same, an' He wants ever'one to know how to git thar.'" He paused, lowered the Bible to hold it open before him and looked at the men, "What muh momma tol' me was I had to know some things and she said fust, was to know I was a sinner," he chuckled, looked around at the men and said, "Even when I was knee high to a grasshopper, I knowed that!" The men laughed, nodding to one another and agreeing with Jeremy.

"Then she said, 'what'chu don't seem to know is that thar's a penalty, or punishment, for sin,' an' I tol' muh momma, 'I knows dat! You whupped me 'nuff so I cain't fo'get that!'" He chuckled again and feigned rubbing his bottom in remembrance of momma's willow switch. "But she goes on an' says just what it say in this hyar Bible," he pointed to the pages before him, "that God in Jesus paid that penalty, punishment, or whuppin', for me! He done went to the cross an' suffered, bled, an' died! All for me!" He paused, scowled and pointed to each of the men, "An' he done it fo' you! An' when He done it, he done it in full an' that means they ain't nuthin' we can do to add to what he done -- not prayers, church goin', good deeds, nuthin'! He done it all!" He shouted the words, held his Bible high, and repeated, "He done it all!"

He paused, lowered his voice and added, "Now… whut most folks miss out an' don't know an' don't do, is to know that what He did on the cross paid for my sin an' yours, an' when He done dat, he paid for the gift of eternal life! Paid fo' it in full!" He moved about, looking at the men, "My momma made me memorize these verses an' here in Romans 6:23 His book says, 'The wages o' sin is death! But the gift of God is eternal life through Jesus Christ our Lord.'"

"Now men, what I wan'chu to remember is gittin' ta' Heab'n is like gittin' a ticket, but that thar ticket is free! Paid fo' by Jesus! But, and now this is th' impo'tant thing, like any gift, you have to git it! Or receive it! An' if you ain't received it, you ain't got it! But God has a ticket or gift fo' you, an' all you gots to do is ask Him fo' it! So," he moved side to side, looking directly at each man, "How you gonna git it? You ask fo' it and how do you do that? Prayer, muh friend, just go to Him in prayer, ax fo' Him to fo'give yo' sin, come into yo' heart, and save you, an' He'll save you by givin' you that free gift of eternal life like it says in the Book!"

He paused, stood up straight and looked around, spoke rather softly, "Men, what we doin' is dangerous bizness, we already had one man bad hurt, 'nother'n almost kilt, and we just gettin' started. Life, death, Heab'n, Hell, ain't nuthin' to take chances with. Now, if'n you wants to make sure that if'n sump'in happens an' you get kilt, an' you wanna make sure of Heab'n, you gots to pray an' ask God for that gift o' eternal life. Ain't got nuthin' to do with nuthin' else, just you an' God, an' you can do it anytime, cuz He's always listenin'. So, that's all I gots to say. Let's us pray together, an' we'll git on with our bizness."

He motioned for every man to close his eyes and bow his head, and Jeremy began to pray. He asked God for His understanding, and that He would lead every man there into that place where he would pray and ask for forgiveness and to accept that gift of salvation or eternal life. He asked for guidance and protection for all the men and for their journey. He concluded with an "Amen," and heard several of the men echo his words.

He lifted his head, looked at the men with a broad smile and said, "Thank you fo' listenin' this mawnin! Now let's git goin', we be burnin' daylight!"

CHAPTER 20

FORT CHURCHILL

From the park near Leavitt Falls, they followed the West Walker River as the trail rode the shoulder above the short canyon before dropping into a long wide grassy valley. By taking a cut through the hills on the north and passing over a high-country saddle, they dropped into the valley of Mill Creek and followed it out of the hills to the valley of the same West Walker River. Charlie had known of the over-the-hills route that took them away from the wagon road and the river but saved them several miles and by the end of the day, they were in a wide green valley that the river and its tributaries had carved eons ago.

Five more days brought them through another canyon along the West Walker River, north through a wide green valley, and across a stretch of scablands to the Carson River. They pushed the herd onto a stretch of sage and bunchgrass in a bend of the river, allowing the horses access to water and using the river to keep the herd together but with room to graze. Eli directed Jeremy to park the wagon midway between the bends and had the men use the available rope and sage to erect a bit of a fence to keep the horses together.

Most of the drovers had gathered near the cook wagon when Eli turned to Mateo and Charlie, "I'm goin' on across to the fort and talk to the commandant. Sheridan said if any of the companies needed remounts, to sell 'em and bring him the rest, long's we didn't leave too many behind." He glanced to the sun, looked around at the available graze, "We've got a couple hours daylight left and the graze is a little skimpy, we'll probably head out in the morning." He looked at Jeremy setting up his cook wagon and asked, "You needin' any supplies? We might be able to get what you need from the fort yonder."

"Nah, boss, I think we alright. But I'll give it another check, and if'n we does, I'll let'chu know."

"Alright. I'm going over now, but we can always make a quick buyin' run if we need."

"Yassuh, boss," replied Jeremy, grinning at Eli, knowing he did not like being called 'boss.'"

Eli shook his head, reined Rusty around and started to the river crossing where two narrow sandbars showed in the middle of the flow and a gravelly bottom made easy crossing. It was evident this crossing had been used many times, probably by the troops at the fort and supply wagons or even settlers visiting. As Rusty came from the water he climbed the slight rise of the bank and stepped out toward the fort.

Eli stood in his stirrups as he looked over the fort. He counted about twenty buildings, all adobe plus wood frames, the barracks were long and two storied, while the other buildings, officer quarters, sutler, headquarters were sporting fresh painted identifying signs. A tall flag-pole, standing in the middle of the square parade ground, had the thirty-seven star nation's flag waving in the breeze. Eli glanced around the buildings as he neared and headed toward the headquarters building. He stepped down, slapped Rusty's rein around the hitchrail and opened the door and stepped in to the two room building.

"Wha'chu want?" growled a crusty looking three stripe sergeant with five hash marks on his sleeve as he sat at a desk and looked up at Eli.

Eli paused, looked at the man, looked around the office and asked, "Who's the commandant?"

"Major Joseph Stewart, why?"

"I would like to see him."

"Like I said, wha'chu want?"

Eli placed both hands on the edge of the desk and leaned toward the weathered sergeant, "Tell him Lieutenant Colonel Elijah McCain, on assignment from General Sheridan, would like to see him!" stated Eli, glaring at the gruff enlisted man. Eli breathed deep, leaned a little closer and added, "NOW!"

The sergeant had started to lean back as Eli neared, and when Eli barked, he fell over backwards, the chair slipping from under him as he flailed around, trying to get to his feet. He finally stood, saluted, "Yes Sir!" and turned on his heel and went to the door to the next room and pushed in and reported loud enough for Eli to hear, "Sir! Lieutenant Colonel Elijah McCain is here to see you, sir!"

"McCain? Where's he from?"

"Said he's on assignment for General Sheridan, Sir."

"Send him in sergeant."

"Yessir." The weather-beaten sergeant clicked his heels, spun around and stepped into the outer office and standing at attention, declared, "The major will see you now, sir!"

Eli kept his stoic expression, nodded to the sergeant and walked briskly past him and into the office and shut the door behind him. He looked at the man behind the desk who was standing and frowning at the appearance of a man who professed to be an officer but was not in uniform.

Major Stewart motioned for Eli to be seated, seated himself and with elbows on his desk he asked, "What can I do for you," and paused, then added, "Colonel?"

Eli grinned, "That is or was my rank. I separated from the service after the war, but I've maintained my contacts. Your sergeant was a little impertinent and I just wanted to see him snap-to a little." He chuckled, "But the reason I'm here, I have a herd of horses across the river and I'm taking them to General Sheridan, but he said if any forts we passed had need, to let you have some in exchange for a signed voucher. Do you have need of any remounts, Major?"

"Well, no, no we don't. We've been able to keep supplied from the ranchers in the area. They were used to supplying horses for the Pony Express and now we're the only buyer in this part of the country, so they're quite willing to sell to us as we have need."

"That's fine, Major. Just wanted to ask, keep everybody happy, you know how that goes."

"I do, yessir, I do." He paused, frowned, "You say you're taking them to General Sheridan, isn't that a bit far? St. Louis should be able to get horses easy enough."

"He's not at St. Louis. They've moved the headquarters to Fort Hays, which is still a long way east, but..." he shrugged, then added, "Have any Indian trouble lately?"

The major shook his head, "Not lately. And if you ask the men of the troop, they almost wish they had some. They often complain that this is the most boring post they've ever had."

"What about further east?"

"Which way are you going?"

"We're taking the old Pony Express route, what some used to call the Emigrant Trail."

"Around here, the Washoe have all gone to the reservation and haven't been any trouble. But the further east you go, you might run into some Paiute, Shoshone, even some Goshute, and of those all but the Goshute could cause problems. Now, they all profess to be peaceable, but…" he shrugged.

"But nothing in particular, no special uprisings, conflicts?"

"Not that I've heard," replied the major. "It's been so peaceful, I got word they might be shutting this post down entirely," he shook his head, "can't really blame 'em."

"I've seen that all over the west, but they're still having Indian problems in the Rockies and will probably keep those posts manned until they get some semblance of peace. I know they've been working on peace with the Sioux, Blackfeet, Crow and others, but you just never know. By the way, I'm also looking to buy another wagon, some water barrels, maybe a four-up of mules. Any ideas?"

"You might try Buckland's Station. That's a stop for the overland stagecoach and was a stop on the Pony Express. He knows the stage will be goin' outta business soon's the railroad gets done so he might have something that'll suit you."

"Thanks major." Eli nodded, stood and extended his

hand, "It's been a pleasure. I wish you luck with your post and your future wherever it may be."

"Here's hoping," replied the major, standing and shaking hands with his visitor. "And good luck to you as you have a long road ahead of you, but even at that, I do sort of envy you. At least you won't get bored!" he chuckled.

"Boredom is something we know nothing about," replied Eli, grinning and turning on his heel to exit the commandant's office. He nodded to the grump behind the desk and left the office. He glanced around the post, thinking about how it might soon be closed down, and shook his head, thinking of all the troopers that would be shipped to a new location, mounted up and reined Rusty around to return to the herd.

CHAPTER 21

DESERT

"All the express stations had water, some of 'em had a well, others were near a stream, but cuz o' the horses, they had to have water," explained Charlie.

Eli shook his head, "Yeah, but...that was a few years back an' there's no tellin' what happened with all them. The streams you can count on, mostly, but wells...I've known natives to dump the bodies of their enemies into the wells to ruin the water. Won't be the first well that served as a grave for some white men."

"But we can't carry 'nuff water for a thousand horses," stated Charlie, looking from Eli to Mateo and Jubal.

Jubal asked, "How much water can we carry in the extra wagon?"

"Six barrels, that'd be shy of four hundred gallons, and no, that's not enough for a thousand horses, but it might be enough to keep most of 'em from dyin' till we could get to water or..." he shrugged. "I don't want to count on the extra water, but I'd feel a lot better havin' it with us."

Eli and the others were gathered by the cook wagon and were waiting for Joshua, Juan Bandini and Pete Staples to finish filling the barrels and bring the wagon to the camp. Eli had struck a good deal with Buckland for the wagon and a four-up of mules and harness and the barrels. The plan was to get an early start and try to make it across much of the dry land before the heat of the day, and maybe even on to the next stop which Eli hoped would be Wildcat Station, a freight station near the Wildcat Scarp below Carson Sink. The men were standing around the tailgate of Jeremy's cook wagon where Eli had his newly acquired map laid out for them to examine. "I got this from Major Stewart, and he said they found it to be pretty accurate. This," he pointed to an "X" to the right of their location near the fort, "is where the Wildcat Freight Station is, they've got good water and graze and I'd like to make it that far tomorrow. I know it's a bit further than what we've been doin' but we need to be near water and they've got it."

————

JOHN SWAIN, with his splinted and bound broken leg, insisted on driving the water wagon and he would broker no argument from Eli. "Well, John, if you think you're up to it, but if it starts gettin' the better of you, you flag one of us down and we'll get you some relief."

"I'll do that, boss," he answered, grinning. Eli suspected the crew had let it be known that Eli did not like being called 'boss' so they would use it whenever they thought they could get away with it, and Eli played along, usually chuckling after he turned away from the perpetrator.

The grey light at the eastern horizon made silhouettes of the few trees and occasional butte that stood before them and Eli looked around as the men, having worked the edges off their chosen mounts for the day, took their places. Mateo would take John Swain's place at point with Pete Staples, while Jim Perry and Pedro Portola were lead swing, Hipolito Bouchard and Juan Bandini were rear swing, and Jubal and Joshua were the flank riders. Junipero Borremeo and Miguel Fages took their turn on the drag. Eli swung aboard Rusty, looked at Grey who stood nearby, and gave the high sign and called out, "Move 'em out!" and put heels to Rusty and headed into the grey light in the east, following the trail of the cook wagon and Charlie Two Toes.

The point men and swing riders did their best to keep the herd away from the flanks of the hills on the south edge of the flats. The alkali deposit was deeper at that edge and by keeping them close, but about a quarter mile or so away, the alkali was not as deep, but it still made the crossing of the sandy flats difficult. The soft soil and white alkali made a fine dust that made breathing difficult, even though the men had scarves over their faces. The tromping of a thousand horses churned up a wispy cloud of tawny colors and the horses struggled with every footfall stirring up more dust.

After eight to ten miles of the dust cloud dragging along behind, they neared the edge of the buttes and the remains of another express station, Hooten Wells. Fortunately, Eli waited at the stone pool of fresh water, and as the horses smelled it, they quickened their pace, but Eli stepped away, climbed back aboard Rusty and left the jostling and shoving to the point men and swing riders. The horses crowded around the water, drank their fill and splashed their nuzzles in the water to clean their nostrils, then moved aside for those behind them. When the last of the horses had their fill, there was no more than a couple inches of water left in the bottom of the big stone tank, but it had served its purpose.

The men had washed their mounts nostrils out with wet scarves, taken their own drink from their canteen, but let their mounts crowd in with the others to drink their fill, and now swung back aboard and started the herd into the low rolling hills. There were a couple wagon roads into the buttes, but Eli and the herd followed the tracks of Charlie and the cook wagon and were soon in the middle of what Eli thought of as wasteland. The flats showed nothing but stunted sagebrush, greasewood, cholla and prickly pear cacti, clumps of bunch grass and fescue and rabbit brush, and dry land as far as he could see.

It was mid-morning, and the temperature was rising. The cloudless sky offered no reprieve, but in the distance to the east, dark-bellied clouds were bunching together and gave a glimmer of hope. Dark red jagged basaltic rocks littered the peaks and shoulders of many of the hills, telling of long-ago volcanic activity in this land. By late afternoon, they broke from the hills to face another long flat with the white of alkali painting the land. But the clouds now brought a little relief before them as the sun bore down from behind them. Green showed among the sage and greasewood, rabbit brush was strutting its spring costume and the grasses were showing green. It was a relief and gave a tempting invitation to cross over to make the planned stop at the Wildcat Station where fresh water waited.

Eli was well ahead of the herd and took to the hills that sided the second alkali flat. He moved Rusty through the scattered basaltic rocks and followed a ridge to the crest of a tall butte. He stepped down, field glasses in hand and sat on a rock to have a look-see at the land before them. As he scanned the flanks of the hills and the flats before him, movement to the side caught his attention and he turned slightly to see a bunch of pronghorn working their way through the bottom of a draw below him, heading to higher country.

Eli grinned, moved below the crest and went to his gear to retrieve his Spencer. He bellied down, crawled back to the crest and slowly worked his way over to see the easy walking bunch of antelope below. He picked out a young buck, noted another behind him, and zeroed in on his first choice. He drew a breath, let some out and slowly squeezed off his shot. The big Spencer bucked and roared, and the bullet flew true, taking the buck just behind his front leg in the lower chest and drove the animal to the ground. He quickly jacked another round, cocked the hammer and looked for another target, but the entire bunch of ten fleet-footed animals had disappeared, leaving the downed buck behind. Eli chuckled, swapped the Spencer for his Winchester Yellow Boy, and leading Rusty behind, started down the slope to get the fresh meat. He lay the dressed out carcass, wrapped in the skin and bagged, atop the packs of the grey, tied it down and mounted up.

When he came from the hills, he met up with Mateo, riding point for the herd, and nodded, nudged Rusty to a trot and caught up with the men and said, "We should make Wildcat 'fore dark." He looked at the sky, appreciated the heavy clouds and the cooler air, "And if we're lucky, we might get a little rain."

Mateo looked at Eli, shook his head, "You have not been in the desert during a rain storm?"

"No, can't say as I have."

"It can be ver' bad. The adobe soil, she won't absorb

the water, it stands and becomes very slick and sticky, hard to travel. We must get to the station before the rain comes."

"I would say it's about five, six miles to the station. Think we'll be alright?" he looked at Mateo, glanced to the sky, and back.

Mateo did the same and lifted his hand to feel the air, looked at Eli, and with his hand outstretched, palm down, wiggled it side to side and grinned, "*Tal vez,* maybe," and chuckled. But as he spoke, the low-lying clouds in the east let loose with jagged lances of lightning and pulled the plug on the curtain of rain.

CHAPTER 22

REPTILES

At Eli's signal and shout the men pushed the herd into a trot, then into a gallop. With Eli, Mateo and Pete Staples in the lead, they were in a race to the Wildcat Station. Most horses love to run, and these had yet to stretch out. With noses in the wind, manes flying, and tails up like flags on a clipper ship they ran into the wind. Rusty was in the lead, and he was not about to let any other animal see anything but his tail. Eli lay along the big stallion's neck, and he encouraged the long legged claybank with every step. The thunder of the herd seemed to shake the very ground they ran across. Keeping to the flank of the buttes on the south, and avoiding the dusty alkali flats on the north, they threaded the needle and trampled sage, rabbit brush, greasewood, and bunch grass, leaving behind a wide swath of churned soil.

After about a mile, Eli slowed the stallion and taking their cue from the leader, Mateo and Pete began to slow and crowd the herd together to slow them as well. The horses tossed their heads, lifted their feet high, and enjoyed the cooler air coming at them from the approaching storm. Mateo moved up beside Eli, "How far, señor?"

"After we round that point," began Eli, motioning to the point of the buttes that jutted from the south, "I'm guessin' it's about two more miles."

Mateo looked at the clouds and the sheet of rain that angled down from the black underbelly, nodded, "The storm, it is there already. We cannot run the horses in the rain, the adobe, too slick!"

"We'll walk them, but we need to keep them moving until the rain hits, maybe a trot, but we have to keep them controlled."

The herd rounded the point and stretched out toward the station just as the rain began to fall. It was not a heavy rain at first, and the horses relished the cool wash and kept their pace steady, the point men leading the way. With the shoulders of the buttes on the right, the flats on the left, they were easily controlled with the swing and flankers on the flats side doing most of the work. When the station raised up from the sage and showed itself through the rain, Eli grinned broadly, twisted around in his saddle to see the point men coming and lifted his hat to wave, "We're here!" he shouted, but knew he probably could not be heard.

As they neared the station, the men started circling them around, letting them bunch up in the lee of the butte behind the station, and watched the horses slipping and sliding in the muck of the adobe. The horses felt the goo under their feet and stepped lightly, watching the ground and puddles of muddy water as they moved. In short order, all stood quiet, heads down, letting the rain drip from their necks, faces, and backs, yet basking in the cool wet wash-off.

Eli went to the front of the station building, but saw it had been abandoned, the door standing ajar, windows broken out, rain dribbling from the sod roof, but he stepped down and pushed the door aside as he stepped inside. It was far from weatherproof, but it was more shelter than the few juniper and piñon trees around. A table was tipped on its side against the back wall, a pair of bunks were stacked against one wall and a metal stove was cocked on its side against the corner of the back wall. Eli looked around, letting his eyes adjust to the dim light and reached for the table, started to lift it up, but a hiss and a movement made him jump back, dropping the table back. He stepped forward, looking carefully around, grabbed a part of a bunk leg and pushed at the table, heard the hiss again and saw the biggest Gila monster he ever imagined. It was about two feet long, fat, with its black and orange beaded skin, and a tongue flicking in and out as it stared at Eli, hissing and snapping and showing his jagged teeth.

Eli started back-stepping toward the door, when the hum and rattle came from beside the bunks. He looked to his right to see a big, coiled diamond back rattlesnake, poised to strike, his tongue flicking at the moist air and watching Eli with beady little eyes as he feigned a strike that made Eli stumble backwards and fall out the door, wide-eyed, kicking his way free of the doorway, watching to see if either of his most dreaded nightmares were following.

Mateo saw him scampering and came running, "What is it?" as he snatched his pistol from the holster and looked at the open door.

"Snake! Gila Monster! Big uns!" He pushed himself up from the muddy adobe slosh and wiped his hands together to try to rid them of the sticky clay, always watching the door, waiting for one of the reptiles to come after him. "I hate snakes! And that lizard is worse'n any snake! I ain't never seen one so big!" he growled, shaking his head and breathing heavily. He glanced to Mateo and saw a wide grin then he began to chuckle and laugh as he holstered his pistol.

Mateo did his best to stop laughing and when Pete came over to see what was happening and Mateo pointed at the doorway, laughing, "He saw a rattlesnake!" and chuckled some more.

Pete's eyes flared wide, showing whites, and he looked from Eli to the door, "Snake?! I hate snakes!" and started backing away, and with a glance over his shoulder he left the cabin and the reptiles to the two boss men.

Mateo stopped laughing, "I'm sorry, señor, but…" he shrugged, grinning. "That's the only dry place around. Some of the men are making a bit of a shelter against the one wall of the barn that looks solid, maybe we could sleep there."

"Anywhere, as long as there is nothing with a split tongue!" growled Eli, embarrassed by his show of fear, but he had hated snakes all his life and he saw no need to change.

The rain soon let up, it had not been a gulley-washer, more of a dust-settler, but it was needed and appreciated. They were able to make a dry bed with some scattered grasses and ground covers, and a hot supper and breakfast made the stop worthwhile. The herd had good water from the tanks at the station, compliments of the passing rainstorm, and with an early start, they hoped to make good progress.

Mid-morning saw them passing the Sand Springs Station, and three more days as the sun was setting behind them, they pushed the herd through the town of

Austin, herding them up in a bit of a basin to the east of town. The men went into town in two shifts, Mateo supervising the first group of six with Jeremy and Missy going to the general store to restock, and Eli and the boys taking the rest of the men in the second shift. Each group had about three hours to get a meal and browse the town. They had little need of a bath having stopped by a hot springs the day before and getting a good soaking.

Eli saw an old-timer sitting on a rocking chair with a lop-eared mutt at his side and an empty bench nearby beckoned Eli to stop for a chat. He always took advantage of any opportunity to mine the locals for information about the trail ahead and thought this whiskery faced oldster would have a wealth of it, so he asked, "Mind if I join you?" motioning to the bench.

"Whatever suits ya'," replied the old man, removing the corn-cob pipe from his toothless mouth so he could spit a gob of tobacco to the street, but missed and hit the edge of the boardwalk, which is what he had done many times before as evidenced by the stains on the weathered boards.

Eli sat down in the shade and sat quiet for a moment until the man asked, "You one o' them what stirred up the dust wit' them horses?"

Eli chuckled, "Yup, that was us."

"Whar you goin' wit' so many?" he asked.

"Takin' 'em east to the army. Cavalry remounts for General Sheridan."

The old man nodded, squinting at the dimming light as the sun began painting the western sky. Eli looked at the man, "What can you tell me 'bout the road east? Anything I need to know?"

"It's dry," grumbled the old man, then cackled with a "hehehe. Betcha din't know that!"

"Oh, I knew that. We've eaten enough dust the last several days we could do without any more." He looked at the man, glanced about, "Austin seems to be a bustling town. Growing?"

"Nah, used to was bigger. Back when it was first started, hehehehe," he cackled, "it got started when a pony express rider's horse pawed at the dirt and over-turned a rock what was pure silver! An' then it all started, but the silver strike's peterin' out, folks leavin'. Some been goin' east to a place they's callin' Eureka. Ain't much more there, but them prospectors don't know nuthin' nohow." He chuckled, looked across the street, "Time was, we was so busy an' growin' that hotel yonder, the International they call it, it used to be in Carson City. They put it on wagons and hauled it out hyar! Can you imagine doin' such a stupid thing? They coulda built it easier, but nooo, they wanted that'n. Then they built onto it after that." He pointed with his pipe down the street, "That steeple yonder's on a brick Catholic Church, and they gotta nother'n they call the Methodist church. Reckon they think all these miners that're livin' like the devil needs to get religion!" He spit again, "Course that didn't help Rufus Anderson." He cackled and spat again, looked at Eli, "Them dumb miners, Rufus was guilty of murderin' a fella, they was s'posed to hang him, but they couldn't even do that right. They had 'em a gallows, put the rope on him, but he fell through the trap an' hit the ground! They did that twict! Hehehehe, so they roped him to a chair an' hung him sittin' down! Finally got'er done!" He shook his head, spat another gob, then tried in vain to light his pipe.

Eli stood, nodded to the old man, "Well, it's been good visitin' with you old-timer, but I need to check on my men, get 'em back to camp."

"Tell ol' Phil that Monty said howdy!"

Eli frowned and looked at the man, who nodded and grinned but offered no explanation.

CHAPTER 23

SCRUB-LAND

"Well, you sure made a good call on this," exclaimed Eli, nodding his head to the green valley below their camp. "Those horses are already enjoying it and if we give 'em a couple more days, they'll be so frisky, they'll wanna run all the way to Fort Hays!" he declared, chuckling, as he sipped his coffee. They were sitting around the morning cookfire, enjoying the hot coffee and waiting for Jeremy and Missy to finish their breakfast fixing. It had been eight days of hard, dry, driving across what he could only describe as scrub-lands. "You know, since we left that nice meadow just outside of Austin, this is the first decent graze and water they've had."

Charlie chuckled, "But I have to admit, I'm thankful you had that water wagon. We came mighty close, a couple times, to losing some of those horses," nodding to the herd, lazily grazing in tall grass that was deep enough to tickle their bellies. "Course, those last few stations that still had water served their purpose too.

Egan Canyon, Schell Creek, Antelope Spring, made it easier on the horses and us too," he chuckled.

"Well, we did lose a few, but not nearly what we could have. But as I look at those mountains yonder," pointing with his cup and nodding that to the south, "and that snow that's still up top, makes me feel better 'bout havin' water the rest of the way. There's some dry country across the big basin in what they've been calling Wyoming, but nothin' as bad as what we came through already," explained Eli.

Mateo asked, "I have heard that Wyoming territory has had a lot of Indian trouble, is that true?"

Eli grinned, "I was stationed at Fort Laramie back in the 50's, and they had problems with the Sioux, Cheyenne, Crow, Blackfoot, and others. And I know that Red Cloud of the Oglala Lakota Sioux has been leading his people in a war over the Bozeman Trail and Fort Kearny and others. He was the leader in the Fetterman Fight a little over a year ago when more than eighty troopers were killed. Course that had as much to do with a cocky captain that thought he was better than any natives and got his men into the trouble. But they've been tryin' to make peace and protect the settlers and miners and others."

"You think we'll run into any trouble?" asked Jubal, glancing around the circle of the others.

"I don't think so, but we'll have to be careful and keep watch. Most of the trouble has been further north than where we'll be going, but then..." he shrugged, "there was the battle of Sand Creek that can only be called a massacre. Another pompous soldier that wanted to be in the war, so he made his own, him an' a bunch of volunteers, attacked a village of Cheyenne and Arapaho and killed a bunch of women and children, and of course, made the warriors mad and they fought back. That was back in '64, down in Colorado Territory, south of where we'll be going, but we will be traveling through their territory."

Joshua twisted around, holding his cup of coffee with both hands between his knees, and looked at his pa and said, "So, let me get this straight, for the last four years, there have been fights with the, uh, let me see, the Sioux, Crow, Cheyenne, Arapaho, and who else?"

"That about covers it," drawled Eli, grinning as he sipped his coffee.

"And the Sioux, Crow and maybe others will be to the north of us, and the Cheyenne and Arapaho to the south of us, and we'll be goin' between them?"

"Well now, that's not quite right. The Cheyenne are north, but the Arapaho, Comanche, Kiowa, and Ute are all south of us," explained Eli, trying to keep a stoic expression.

"Oh, so now there are others?" asked Joshua, leaning forward, eyes wide and eyebrows lifted, gripping his cup a little tighter.

Jubal leaned forward and asked, "So, if we get through all that, what natives are in the Fort Hays area?"

"Oh, that's Pawnee country."

Mateo asked, "Why did we leave California?"

Eli chuckled, "The adventure, Mateo, the adventure!" He stood, tossed aside the dregs of the coffee, "Now you all can think about natives, but I'm goin' to breakfast!"

———

"Now, pick a young bull or a cow without a calf. It's early yet, and the cows might not have dropped their calves, so if you're goin' for a cow, pick a skinny one," chuckled Eli. The three men, Eli, Jubal and Joshua were just inside the tree line on the high side of a park that was framed by aspen that were just sprouting their green leaves. They had ridden south of the park where the horses were pastured and gone into the high country and the black timber that held patches of aspen. The white barked trees contrasted with the deep green grasses of the meadow and the herd of elk was filing into the basin, a big cow in the lead as the herd was pushed by a big bull.

"So, how do I pick a young bull, ain't none of 'em got much more'n spikes for antlers?" asked Jubal, down on one knee beside the rough barked ponderosa.

"See that big 'un at the back, the one pushin' the others? That's the herd bull, but the young ones will be at the edges or the back end of the herd. They'll have spikes, but not big ones and they won't be as big or as tough as the herd bull." He glanced from one to the other and told Jubal, "Now wait till your brother's ready and you can both shoot about the same time. The herd'll spook when the first shot it taken."

Jubal was sighting and moving a little with the herd, "I'm ready, you?" he asked, directing his soft spoken words to his brother who was on the far side of the same tree.

Joshua had seated himself and was using both knees to support his elbows as he aimed his Spencer, and replied, "Yeah, do it on three. One, two, three!"

Both rifles roared and bucked, licked out with tongues of fire and grey smoke, and both shooters came to their feet, looking at the scattering herd. One bull staggered and fell, another one was already on the ground, as the rest of the herd charged through the tall grass and disappeared into the aspen grove and into the black timber beyond.

"Good shootin'!" said Eli, grinning as he looked at the downed animals. He chuckled, "Now comes the hard part! Grab your horses and let's get started."

It was only about eighty yards to where the carcasses lay, and Eli asked, "Either one of you done any guttin'?"

Jubal frowned, "Of course we have. We sure don't look like we been starvin', do we?" he laughed, patting his middle and glancing to his brother, who grinned in response.

"Then let's get to work. You open 'em up, an' I'll get the grey ready to pack. He won't be able to carry it all, so we'll make smaller bundles with the hides. Put the back straps, and the hind quarter meat in the first stack, then cut the meat from the bones and stack it together. Uh, we might take the livers and hearts too, they can be mighty tasty when cooked right and I think Jeremy can handle that."

When they rode back into camp with bundles behind each saddle and the grey loaded heavy, they were greeted by a grinning Jeremy who said, "Fresh meat! That's what we been needin', yassuh. Didja get the innards?"

Eli chuckled, "Right there on top," nodding to the pack horse and the bundles atop the pack saddles.

Jeremy started unloading as the men stepped down and helped to unburden the horses. Mateo walked near, frowning, and Eli looked at him, cocked his head to the side a little and asked, "What's wrong?"

"We had some visitors, Indians. They said they were Unkagarits band of the Goshute. They, and there were about eight or ten of them, said they must be paid for us to cross their land. They said all that," he pointed to the east flats that lay before them, "is their land."

"And just what did they want to be paid?"

"One hundred horses."

"A hundred?!" asked Eli, incredulous. "They want a hundred horses? No, huh uh, not a hundred. We don't even know if that's their land?" pleaded Eli, shaking his head.

Charlie stepped near, "It is not their land, but we will cross some of their land when we turn north."

"What do you think we should do, Charlie?"

"Talk to them. They will be back, but don't pay the hundred. Maybe ten, or…" he shrugged.

CHAPTER 24

NORTH

"That's the upper end of the Deep Creek Range an' we're headin' into the Snake Valley," stated Charlie, nodding to the mountains on their right that were catching the first beams of the rising sun that was doing its best to paint the faces of the mountains that held the last of spring snow in shades of pink and orange.

"Snake Valley? Don't tell me it's called that because of a lot of snakes!" responded Eli, shaking his head and frowning.

"Why else?" chuckled Charlie. He pointed to some rocks, "That there's what's left of Cañon Station. The next one's Willow Springs."

"Good water?"

"Last time I was through here it was, but..." he shrugged, a cock-eyed grin showing on his face as he looked sidelong to Eli. He nodded down the road, "Mebbe they can tell you different."

Eli looked where Charlie directed, to see several riders spaced across the road and knew these were the

Goshute warriors he had expected to see earlier. The two men did not slow, and Eli slipped his Winchester from the scabbard to lay it across his pommel. Charlie did the same with his Henry and both men held the weapons with thumbs on the hammers. Although they carried their rifles with cartridges already chambered, the weapons would not fire until they cocked the hammers. Eli was not expecting trouble from these natives for they were known as peaceful people, but he also knew every tribe had their renegades.

The two men reined up before the seven warriors, four of whom had rifles standing on their thighs with their thumbs on the hammers, two had war lances with feathers and what appeared to be scalplocks, and one held a bow with arrow nocked. All sat with stoic expressions and one man moved slightly forward, "We said 100 horses! Where are the horses?" growled the leader, scowling at Eli and Charlie.

Eli cocked his head to the side, looked at each of the warriors and glanced to Charlie, then back to the leader. "I am Eli. Those horses go to the Army. We will take them all to the army of General Sheridan. This is not your land. Your land is far to the south. We travel the way of the Pony Express and the Overland Stage and have no need to give you horses." He used sign language as he spoke to ensure that all of the warriors understood what he said.

"You will pay 100 horses, or we will take all of the horses!" growled the leader.

"The only way you will get horses is if two," and he held two fingers before him, then pointed at each of the warriors, "of your warriors go with our scout to find the water our horses need. They will go all the way to Fort

Bridger in Wyoming Territory, far past the great lake of salt."

The leader frowned, looked at his men, then back to Eli, who had casually and surreptitiously moved his rifle so that it pointed directly at the leader. Eli cocked the hammer, and the ratcheting sound was loud in the stillness. The warrior's eyes flared, and he looked at Eli, who was grinning. The leader snarled, started to bring his rifle to bear and Eli shook his head, "Don't move!"

"We have more men, you will both be killed," warned the leader of the Goshute.

Eli grinned, "But you won't live long enough to know that. The first bullet will kill you, then I'll fire a second time and kill that one," pointing with his chin to the warrior on the leader's left who held the war lance. "And my partner," nodding slightly to Charlie, "will kill that one," nodding to the warrior on the leader's right, "And that one also," referring to the next man. "So that means that four of you will be dead. Are any number of horses worth the lives of four warriors?"

"You will be dead also!" growled the leader.

Eli grinned, "And my sons, who are with the herd, will take all the men and follow the rest of your warriors back to your village and kill all your women and old people and anyone else."

"How many horses you give for scouts?" asked the leader.

"Two. One for each scout, but only if the scouts go all the way to Fort Bridger, that's more than two hands of days there and two hands of days to return, maybe more."

"No! We go!" declared the leader and jerked the head of his mount around and forced his way past his warriors to lead them away from the road.

Eli and Charlie watched as they turned south to cut across the sagebrush and greasewood flats, raising a dust cloud as they disappeared into the foothills. Charlie looked at Eli, shook his head slightly and chuckled, "They thought for sure they were gonna buffalo you, but didn't happen. I kinda figgered you had a steel rod for a backbone." He chuckled some more, nudged his mount onward and Eli sided him as they rode in silence, watching the rising sun bathe the flats in brassy light.

They made an early nooning at Willow Springs, with all the horses getting ample water and naturally snatched as much grass as possible, then pushed on to the Boyd Station. With the strong stone building and deep well kept in good repair by Bid Boyd who still resided there, they had no lack of good water. With the horses well-watered, they pushed on to Fish Springs and made camp by the light of dusk. The men stretched out their bedrolls under the three big oak trees that stood near the station house, but the station housed the passengers from the stage that had stopped for the night.

Three days later, they circled up the herd on the site of what had been the military post called Camp Floyd. The remains of several adobe structures showed but none were complete and usable. Nearby was the Stagecoach Inn and Eli and Charlie had made arrangements for the men, including Jeremy and Missy, to take their evening meal at the Inn and Eli, Charlie, Jubal and Joshua took rooms for the night.

"A bath?!" asked Charlie, frowning at Eli, "You're paying for a bath?"

Eli chuckled, "That's right. It's a hot bath and I'm going to enjoy it immensely!"

Charlie looked at the twins, "You too?"

Jubal chuckled, "You might give it a try Charlie. You

might like it, and," with a glance to his brother and father, "we would like to *see you* give it a try, for *our* benefit Charlie."

"Your benefit, what'chu mean?" he feigned surprise and not understanding but lifted his arm to sniff his armpit, made a face and turned away, "Oh."

———

WITH THE OQUIRRH MOUNTAINS on their left and the Lake mountains to their right, they headed the herd into the rising sun to split the mountains and make for the Jordan River. With the road bending to the north, for them to cross Cedar Valley, it was with the sun at their back before they came to the flats with the Jordan River. They dropped off the flat-tops into the valley of the Jordan and the horses were glad to stop in the deep grasses.

As they sat near the cookfire sipping their coffee, Eli explained, "That fella I was talkin' to at the Stagecoach Inn, said another day past the Jordan River and we should make the mouth of Emigration Canyon. Another couple days would see us to a little settlement called Henefer, maybe a little further to Echo. But then…then we go into Echo Canyon, another long and narrow canyon, but I was assured that there are no high-up roads, it's all in the canyon bottom!"

It was the beginning of the fourth day when they started into Echo Canyon. The south side was mostly scrub oak, chapparal, and red rock, with knobby hills that stood high over the canyon. The north slopes showed red rock in stratified layers, intermingled with chapparal and topped with juniper and piñon that freckled the rolling crowns. Echo Creek twisted its way through the willows to make its way southwest to exit the canyon.

Then further into the canyon, the red rock bulked and pushed away the lesser soils, but the hills rose over a thousand feet above the canyon floor. For most of the day, the clatter of horses hooves bounced across the narrow canyon, continually repeating and repeating as the more than one thousand horses trailed through the canyon that was usually no more than eight hundred feet wide, but wide enough the herd was not strung out more than usual.

A little before mid-day, Echo creek merged with two creeks, one from the west hills and one from the east. The canyon widened and grass was abundant, so Jeremy had set up his wagon for nooning, and the rest was welcomed by all. By late afternoon, they exited the canyon and had caught up with Jeremy once again, and he was grinning and singing as he finished making the cornbread biscuits to cook in the Dutch ovens.

Charlie stepped down from his mount, looked at Eli who was leaning against the cook wagon and said, "We'll be in Wyoming territory 'bout mid-mornin' tomorrow."

Eli grinned and nodded, "Thought so, and I'll be glad to get out of this desert country!"

CHAPTER 25

"So, have you boys corresponded with your ladies since we left?" asked Eli, looking over his coffee cup to the two young men.

Jubal grinned, "We hoped to send 'em a telegram when we get to Fort Bridger. Seein' as how it's a military fort, they'd probably have a telegraph."

"An' just what're you gonna tell 'em?"

"Oh, where we are, a general idea when we'll get to Fort Hays, and then on to Louisville."

"And when are you thinkin' we'll get to Fort Hays?" drawled Eli, a bit of a grin tugging at his cheeks.

"Didn't you say we'd get there about the end of June, first of July?" asked Joshua, leaning forward with his coffee cup between his legs, elbows on his knees.

"Yeah, 'bout that, give or take a week or so."

Jubal looked contemplative as he asked, "How long you think it'll take us to get to Louisville?"

Eli grinned, "Depends on the railroad. It'll go through St. Louis and on to Louisville, so I reckon once you're on the train, three, four days, give or take."

The boys looked at one another, grinning, "That sounds good, don't it?" asked Jubal as he chuckled and looked at his brother with a wide smile.

"But how are the ladies goin' to get there?"

"That we don't know," replied Jubal, his grin turning into a somber frown, "'fore we left, their Ma was talkin' 'bout them takin' a stage as far as they could go 'till they reach the railroad, but she also mentioned taking a Clipper Ship down the coast, take the wagons over the isthmus and another ship up to New Orleans. Then take a river boat up to the Ohio and then another'n up to Louisville. It's further, but easier goin' 'ceptin' for the crossing of the Isthmus of Panama."

Joshua leaned forward, glanced to his brother then to his father, "I think she'll insist on going by boat, and I can't blame her, it would be easier for them, and she said it might even be cheaper."

"So, they might get there well before you do?"

Jubal shrugged, "Might."

"You might drop a letter to the folks at the farm about them coming, just in case, or even a telegram."

"Who's there?" asked Joshua.

"Your Aunt Patience and her husband, your Uncle Ephraim. Their place, as you know, is right beside ours and they have always helped out when I was gone. And of course, there's the trainer, George Washington Corbin, his wife, and his two boys also work the place. They might have more working there now, but..." he shrugged.

Jubal looked at his brother and back to his Pa, "We'll send a telegram to Uncle Ephraim."

"Then let's get movin'!" declared Eli, standing and tossing aside the dregs of his coffee.

They made an easy crossing of the Bear River, stopped for nooning, and pushed on into the hills. Eli was far out on a scout, taking some time to himself. As he looked around at the rolling tawny hills, some with layers of rimrock stacked in veins that broke the monotony of the smooth hills and the endless buffalo grass that waved in the breeze that moved unhindered across the vast plains. He considered his boys, he was proud of them, hopeful for them, and beginning to trust them more than before. They were showing themselves as men, taking responsibility as needed, being considerate of others and always willing to do more than their share. He was starting to believe they were becoming the men both he and their mother had long hoped for, and the thought of their pending marriage, well, they would have a lot to learn about that. Eli chuckled to himself, then sobered as he considered his own life, what would he do when they finished this drive?

So much of his life had been spent in uniform and he had little time or reason to think about his future and the rest of his life. It was too easy just to do what his orders dictated, fulfill his responsibility, and keep his head down. The main reason he took his separation was because of Margaret's illness and her concern for the boys. Had he stayed in, he would probably be a full colonel or maybe even a general by now, and who knows where he would be stationed. Probably somewhere in the west, what with the ongoing Indian trouble.

But he had also considered a different life when he met Donna and helped her buy that restaurant in Walla Walla, she was probably expecting him to return someday, and well...he chuckled. As he allowed his mind to wander, he was brought back to the present when Rusty stopped suddenly, lifted his head and had his ears pricked as he looked at the edge of a bluff before them. There was something there that caught his attention, and it was something he did not like. The big stallion tossed his head, snorted, and turned to look at Eli as if to ask, "Well? Now what?"

He leaned back and took his binoculars from the saddle bags and began to scan the bluff and the talus slope at the end. The rimrock probably prevented anyone from being up top, but Rusty was looking at the point of the bluff where scattered piñon and juniper offered cover. Eli nudged Rusty to a close juniper and stood in his stirrups to watch the bluff. Within moments, several riders showed themselves coming from the back side of the bluff, natives, no pack horses, no women, looked to be a raiding party. He counted a dozen warriors, most with rifles, only a couple with lances and shields.

If they had not already spotted the horse herd, they would soon enough, and Eli knew the herd would be a tempting target, for most plains tribes counted their wealth in the number of horses owned, and especially those that had been stolen in a raid against an enemy. From what he remembered from his time at Fort Laramie, he guessed these to be Shoshone, but he also thought they were making peace with the army, yet he knew that young men among any of the native peoples made their mark or passage to manhood as a warrior by taking plunder from an enemy and nothing was more prized than horses. And with most of the plains tribes, a young man bought a bride with horses, making it all the more tempting, even if the chiefs and leaders were negotiating a peace treaty.

Eli looked around, behind him was a long dry gulch, and on the far side, the flank of a high butte that would make a good promontory for watching the raiding party. He backed Rusty toward the gulch, reined him around and nudged him over the edge. They moved down the gulch a short distance and when a cluster of juniper offered cover, they climbed the embankment, moving around the point of the butte and seeing a possible route for ascent, pointed Rusty to the depression and with the grey close behind they made the climb easily. Once atop, Eli slipped to the ground, bellied down and crawled to the edge to look for the raiding party.

As he watched, a lone rider came at a gallop from the hills to the west, the general direction of the herd. He rode up to the party, stopped and began gesturing, pointing and talking very animatedly. Eli shook his head, knowing the scout had undoubtedly seen the herd and with its size more than he could describe, his excitement was contagious, and the other warriors crowded around him and became very excited, many gesturing by lifting their weapons overhead, some even shouting their war cries. Eli shook his head, watching and wondering. As he crabbed back, a low dust cloud to his right caught his attention and he turned with his binoculars to see what was coming down the road.

A ribbon of white rocked through the thin dust cloud and to the side of the lead wagon, a cavalry troop, looking to be about twenty plus strong, riding with the wagon train of probably fifty wagons. Eli grinned, turned his glasses back to the natives, who were obscured from the view of the wagons and troopers, and had not yet spotted the oncoming wagons. Eli turned back to the road that stretched out to the east, calculated a route he could take to reach the troopers before they neared. He grinned as he visually followed the gulch he used before and knew that would take him far enough.

He quickly mounted Rusty, spoke to the grey, and they started off the back side of the butte. They came off the butte, sliding on their rumps, digging in their heels, and fighting to avoid the outcroppings of rock. Once to the bottom, Eli dug his heels into Rusty's ribs and they took off at a gallop, dropped into the gulch and moved as quickly as the twisting gulch would allow, and when near enough, Eli reined Rusty to the embankment and in three lunges, the big claybank topped out, followed closely by the grey and was quickly spotted by the leaders of the troops and the wagons.

Eli saw the commander of the troopers lift his hand in a signal to stop and then rein his own mount toward Eli, with a grizzled sergeant at his side. Eli chuckled, slowed as he approached, came to a sliding stop and nodded to the captain, "Captain -- there's a raiding party of Shoshone warriors just around the point of that bluff yonder," he pointed over his left shoulder, "and I've got a herd of horses coming up the road."

"How many in the party of Indians?"

"I counted about a dozen, then another scout came to report, might be more."

"How many men do you have with your herd?"

"Twelve, counting the cook and his wife. My scout's out ahead."

"Well, we shouldn't have any trouble handling that many…" began the captain and with a second thought, "How do you know they're Shoshone?"

Eli grinned, "Met a few when I served at Fort Laramie, before the war."

The captain frowned, scowled at Eli and asked, "North or South?"

Eli grinned, "Lieutenant Colonel under Sheridan."

The captain nodded, "Then I'll follow your lead. What do you suggest, Colonel?"

Eli reined Rusty around, "Let's just get out front of the wagons, let 'em see you and your men, they'll probably find a reason to return to their village," he replied, grinning.

CHAPTER 26

OVERLAND

With no contact with the natives, apparently the presence of the troopers kept them at bay, it was early afternoon the following day when they neared Fort Bridger. The troopers had continued with the wagons as far as Bear River and planned to return from that point. The intercontinental telegraph system was at Fort Bridger, and Jubal and Joshua were anxious to send the telegrams to both the girls and to the family at Louisville. They were surprised when they had a quick reply from Monterey and as the telegrapher handed it off, he said, "The operator said they were waiting for word from you. This gram was already written and waiting on someplace to send it, so, here you go!" and handed the telegram to Jubal.

The two quickly left the building, sat down on a bench under a big oak tree just outside the telegraphers office and Jubal began to read. "Already underway. Clipper to Isthmus, another to New Orleans. Please send telegram to the office in New Orleans. Plan to take riverboat on to Louisville. Should arrive there late May, early June."

It was signed -- MRS. GENEVIÈVE DEVEREAUX WITH GISÈLE AND GABRIELLE.

They looked at one another, both showing broad grins and laughing. Joshua said, "I knew she'd be coming with 'em!"

Jubal grinned and looked at his brother, "You know why she's coming don't you?"

Joshua frowned, "The wedding, of course."

Jubal chuckled, "I think it's more than that. I think she has designs on our father!" he laughed as he shook his head, grinning at his brother.

"Oh. Wouldn't that be somethin', brothers married to sisters, and…" he laughed, "So, he would be our step-father and our father-in-law!"

————

THE OVERLAND STAGE ROAD, which bore mostly east from Fort Bridger, had parted ways with the Oregon Trail that took to the north and would cross over South Pass, but Eli, familiar with the territory from his many patrols from Fort Laramie, preferred to stay to the south. The Overland was also called the Emigrant Trail, but the California, Mormon, and Oregon Trails also were, on occasion, referred to as the Emigrant Trail or trails. After questioning the commandant at Fort Bridger and knowing the ways of the natives and the progress of the Union Pacific Railroad, he decided to take the route he had originally chosen and that was to follow the Over-land Trail until it divided, the route to the south for the stage line, and due east for the military route which was also used by west-bound settlers.

It was mid-afternoon when they left Fort Bridger and followed the Blacks Fork River which was sided by the Overland Trail. By dusk, they settled down at the confluence of Smith Fork and the Blacks Fork where the grass was deep and plentiful and the terrain flat and with the rivers near, it would be easy to keep the herd gathered close.

Another early start saw them pushing past the Granger Stage Station shortly after sun-up, then at the direction of their scout, Charlie, they cut across country through the buffalo grass and sage, to the Blacks Fork after it bent to the south. Then cutting due east, they soon sided the Green River, followed it south to an easier crossing just above the confluence with Bitter Creek, and followed Bitter Creek for the rest of the day, and all the next day when the creek bent to the south. From the stage station at Granger, many places along the route showed signs of the coming Union Pacific Railroad. A town had been platted out at the confluence of Bitter Creek and Green River, and the stage stations along the road that sided Bitter Creek, some were being converted to stops for the railroad, although still used by the stage line. It was at the Almond Stage Station when Bitter Creek bent to the south and the herd continued to side the meandering creek when the trail turned south with the creek.

It was late the following day when they hove in sight of the stone buildings of Fort LaClede. It was a desolate post, with unreliable water just south of the confluence of Bitter Creek and Antelope Creek. Eli rode ahead and was greeted from the gun tower that adjoined the barracks. "Whats'ur bizness?" called the trooper from high above Eli. Eli shaded his eyes with his hat, looked up at the man, "We're drivin' a herd of horses, you might even see 'em from up there. Want to spend the night hereabouts."

"Ain't much grass right yet, but thar's water n' some graze down by the crick, yonder. You're welcome to it!" replied the trooper.

"What's your outfit, trooper?" asked Eli.

"Comp'ny B, 11th Ohio Volunteer Cavalry, commanded by Cap'n Ridgely."

"Been out here long?" asked Eli, looking up at the trooper who was leaning over the railing to look down at Eli.

"Since 'fore the war! We'ns s'posed to be gettin' relieved or sumpin'. Better happen soon or most o' these fellers are gonna high tail it on back to the green grass of home anyhow!"

Eli chuckled, looking about at the flats showing nothing but sagebrush, with patches of prickly pear and cholla cactus. The nearest tree was about a half-mile away and it was a stunted piñon. "Your captain around?"

"'Spectin' him an' the patrol any time now. They was headed east with a stage. Gotta protect them eastern money folks," he drawled, spat a long stream of tobacco and wiped his chin with his sleeve.

"We'll be makin' camp down by the creek, but if he gets in before I come back, tell him Lieutenant Colonel Elijah McCain would like to meet with him."

The trooper straightened up, adjusted his loosened blouse and appeared to swallow his tobacco as he choked and replied, "Yes sir! Will do, sir!" as he stood at attention.

Eli chuckled, "As you were trooper, I'm not on active duty. But I would like to talk to your captain."

"Yes sir!"

Eli turned to see the approaching cook wagon and

herd, knowing his sons were on point and he stood in his stirrups, motioned them to take the herd to the creek bottom for the night. Jeremy waved as he pulled the wagon into the bottom as well, wanting to be as near the water as possible. The sun was lowering in the west and with no mountains to hide behind, ol' sol appeared to strut his stuff by sending long lances of gold stretching across the western sky and painted a red and orange curtain to rise with a glow that chased away the blues of the hot day. Eli picketed Rusty and Grey within reach of the water and stacked his gear in the lee of the low embankment. He walked to the cook wagon, saw the lid on the coffee pot dancing and lifted the big pot from the hanger that held it over the fire and poured himself a cup that boiled up when it hit bottom. It was blacker than midnight and Eli lifted the cup to take in the aroma of the dark brew, went to a rock and sat down.

Jeremy called out, "Hongry boss?"

"No more'n usual, Jeremy. What's on the menu tonight?"

"Strip steaks from those Antelope Charlie brought in, some Indian taters an' cattail buds, biscuits an' gravy, an' Missy's makin' some bear sign fer desert!"

"So, Missy, do I get to sample some o' that bear sign?"

"Yassuh, jist as soon as they's done, an' that'll be 'bout the time you clean yo' plate!"

"You mean I hafta wash my own plate an' such?" Eli asked, trying his best to look and sound exasperated at the thought.

"Don'chu allus do that?" Missy replied in her squeaky voice and giggling.

"Did I hear someone say something about bear sign?" came a strange voice from behind Eli.

He twisted around to see the uniformed post commandant, Captain Ridgely, who added, "I haven't had a decent donut since I left Ohio!"

"Well, have a seat Captain. Maybe we can feed you and give you a couple for desert, if Missy will allow it." He grinned, looked to Missy and asked, "How 'bout it, Missy. Think you'll have enough to share with the Captain?"

"If'n he ax reeeaal nice, mebbe," she giggled again, nodding to the two men.

The captain seated himself on one of the many flat slabs of rock that were found in the area, most being rejects after the building of the two structures that made up the fort. He leaned back, stretched out his legs and extended his hand to Eli, "I'm Captain Ridgely. My trooper says you're a Lieutenant Colonel?"

"Was. Served with General Sheridan, but I separated shortly after the cessation of hostilities to return home to a dying wife. Since then, I've been traveling over much of this country for one reason or another. Now, we're taking this herd of horses to General Sheridan at Fort Hays."

"Looks to be quite a herd. You've got a job to do, that's for sure. I did not know Sheridan was in Fort Hays," he made the statement as much a question as a comment.

Eli nodded, "They moved the headquarters for the Department of Missouri there and that's where he needs the remounts. So, Captain, have you had much trouble with the natives?"

He grinned, shook his head, "About a year ago, we had quite a skirmish, lost some men, but killed some Indians, and since then they've stayed clear. We take out patrols to guard the stages and any wagon trains, freighters, and such, but we do that as much to allay the boredom as anything."

"Anything else interesting happening?" asked Eli.

"The most exciting thing lately has been seein' a bunch of mustangs led by one impressive black stallion. They came down at night, tried to break out some of our saddle stock, but fortunately the guards were ready for 'em and fired a few shots, scared 'em away."

"When was that?" asked Eli.

"Couple nights ago. They can't be too far, and seein' that herd, he might try to add a few to *his* herd," suggested the captain.

Jeremy stepped out holding the steel triangle and began to sound the clanging to call the men to supper. Eli grinned, looked at the captain, "Join us?"

The captain grinned, "I've been known to do just about anything to get some bear sign!"

CHAPTER 27

MUSTANGS

After gleaning as much as possible from the captain regarding the east bound trail, Eli rolled everybody out well before daylight. He explained, "It's gonna be a hot day and a dry road ahead. Wanna get as far as we can before the sun gets too hot. We might hafta rest in the heat of the day and keep movin' after dark. We'll have a full moon tonight and it might be easier travelin' across these dry plains."

While they were eating supper the night before, an Overland Stage went past the fort and stopped at the stage station just a mile beyond the fort. Eli had asked the captain about the regularity of the stages and understood there would be no more than one or two that might meet them on the road, but Eli also knew that a stage running through a herd of a thousand horses might be a little dangerous. As they gathered for breakfast, Eli looked to Charlie, "Be sure to warn any stages that you see on the road. I know you usually do that, but with the flats as they are, I'd hate to have to do another round-up of spooked horses."

"Will do, as long as they slow down to talk. Sometimes the driver just sees me as an Indian and won't slow."

"Just do what you can and watch for mustangs. The captain said there's a good sized herd with a stallion that likes to raid other herds."

"You want me to catch him?"

"Oh yeah, that's just what we need. A rank stallion that thinks every mare he sees is his!"

Charlie chuckled, "That's what I think when I go to town!"

"No wonder you're always in trouble," chuckled Eli.

———

THEY PASSED the Dug Springs stage station and were approaching Duck Lake station when a rise of dust came from beyond a flat-top mesa to the right of the road. With a flat bottomed dry gulch that carried the road, even a rattlesnake could raise dust, but Eli stood in his stirrups and shaded his eyes against the brassy sky and bold sun to see horses coming around the point of the mesa. The leader of the herd was a big black and he crested a slight rise, reared up to paw at the sky to tell the world he had arrived, and he was the boss of this land. Rusty tensed, began to prance side to side, his head raised, ears pricked as he tossed his head, straining at the bosal and reins held tightly in Eli's hand.

Eli was less than a quarter mile ahead of the herd and the point men were the two gauchos, Hipolito and Pedro, and they had been warned about the mustang stallion and his herd. Eli looked back at the herd, saw Hipolito move away from the leaders, and toward the mustang stallion. Eli reached down to stroke Rusty's neck, trying to calm him, but Rusty saw the stallion as a threat and a challenge, and he wanted to meet that challenge. Rusty pranced, nickered, and when the mustang stallion stopped, looked at the claybank, and reared up again, his whinny was a definite challenge and Rusty answered, rearing up, pawing the air before him and answering with his own counter-challenge. When he dropped to all fours, Eli shook his head and started to swing down and let Rusty have his way, but the big black turned away and charged at an all out run, galloping toward the herd. He drove right into the herd, behind the leaders and the point men, but Hipolito swung around and went after the stallion.

Within moments, Hipolito had cut through the herd and given chase to the stallion that shoved several horses, probably mares, before him, cutting them from the herd. As they broke ranks, Hipolito was behind them and just as the stallion reared up, commanding his captives, the gaucho neared and Eli saw him swing his arm above his head and he knew the gaucho was using his boleadoras, the weapon of his people. He let it fly and suddenly the black stumbled and fell to his chest, the bolas wrapped around his front legs. The stallion fought frantically, kicking with his hind legs and crashing his head on the ground.

Hipolito approached, stepped down, and moved to the stallion from the back above his head. Pedro had joined him, and the two men threw a blanket over the stallion's head, put their weight on his neck and middle, staying out of reach of his hind legs. Within moments, the stallion had stilled, but his breathing was ragged and angry, as Eli came near. Rusty was nickering, a deep chested rumble coming forth, but Eli calmed him and looked at the downed stallion.

"Tie him, secure him, and leave his head covered. We'll wait till the herd passes and you can come back to release him."

"Si, señor, we will do that. Do you want us to round up his herd and add them to ours?" asked Hipolito.

Eli chuckled, "That'd sure make him mad. But no, they've been wild too long and might run off some of ours. Leave 'em. And give us plenty of time to get the herd down the road a piece."

As Eli started to mount up, he saw a dust cloud from beyond the herd, and reckoned another stage was coming. The herd had split, moving to both sides of the road, to let the stage pass but he was sure the driver and passengers were none too happy about the dust they had to endure.

The low rolling hills with the many mesas and flat-top buttes showed the green of spring, even the usual blue sage took on a caste of green. Rabbit brush, grease wood, buffalo grass, gramma, all added to the myriad of hues, and all contrasted with the red of the desert to the north. The road showed a hint of red as it pushed past the stage stations of Duck Lake, Washakie, Sulphur Springs, and finally to the crest of Bridger Pass. It was the highest point on the road, but still rim rocked mesas were layered in the distance, with scattered round top buttes, bluffs with talus slopes, and antelope. Antelope were everywhere, but with their extraordinary eyesight, they seldom came within shooting distance of the scout or the men as they pushed the massive herd across the countryside.

It had been three days since they left Fort LaClede, and another day and a half brought them to the North Platte River. They were beginning to see a few ranches, and a mix of longhorn and cross breed cattle that covered the grassy hillsides. Where there was water, there would be settlers, some would make it, others would leave behind the scars of their heartbreak with bones whitened in the sun and dugouts and log cabins fallen in, but a few would prosper and those that had good grazing land near the river seemed to be making a go of it.

The point men were two vaqueros, Junipero and Miguel, but Mateo rode well ahead, not just scouting the land, but the crossing they were about to make. The road for the stages made a crossing on what appeared to be a shallow stretch with gravelly bottom, but a herd of a thousand horses, all anxious to get their feet wet and even roll in the shallow water, needed more room than a six-up pulling a stage. Mateo rode upstream, looking at the bottom as much as possible, but the water was less than clear, and he knew it was probably from the distant storm they heard the night before. He cautiously checked the footing, looking to the banks and the shallows for any giveaway as to danger. He turned and started downstream or north, passed the stage crossing and the river made a dog-leg bend to the right and the current cut away the bank on the left. He noticed the churning of the water and the muddier look, frowned and started closer, but his horse tossed his head and side-stepped. As he brought his horse under control, he looked at the swirling current and knew the whirlpool was probably bottomed with quicksand. He turned back upstream, went to the crossing and held up his hand to stop the herd.

Mateo spoke to Junipero and Miguel, "There is quicksand below the crossing, at the bend of the river. Keep the herd as far upstream as you can. Jun, I want you to drop out as you cross, stay in the middle of the river and keep the horses away. As the swing and flankers come by, you change off and return to the point."

"Si, Mateo," answered Junipero, and a nod from Miguel served as an affirmative answer.

Mateo swung his mount around and started down the north side of the herd to give the same orders to the swing and flank riders, adding, "Stretch out the herd, keep them close together for the narrow crossing. We will make the crossing as quickly as possible. They can get their drink as they cross."

The crossing was going well, the men kept the horses close and stretched out so they would not crowd one another as they moved across the water, until a big bay gelding that had repeatedly been a trouble maker, pushed past a couple mares, crowding them close to Pete Staples who had been the flanker on the north side, and bulled into Pete's horse, making the sorrel stumble back and splash down into the shallows. Pete stayed aboard the red horse, but the bay gelding crowded past and started downstream, splashing wide and wild. Pete reined his sorrel around and gave chase. He loosed his rawhide riata and built a loop and began swinging it overhead as he neared the renegade. He threw the loop, and it settled over the head of the runaway and Pete immediately dallied the riata around his saddle horn and held tight, allowing the big bay to hit the end of the slack and be jerked back.

The bay stumbled when it hit the end of the slack, staggered sideways, but he was so much bigger than the sorrel under Pete, both horses stumbled and splashed through the current. The bay was dragging the sorrel until Pete saw the whirlpool and he loosed the dally, tossing the riata after the bay who fought free of the current and began climbing the rocky shoal and bank.

But the sorrel did not have good footing and was struggling, and Pete knew they had hit the edge of the quicksand. He looked around with wide eyes, searching for an escape, but drove his feet deep in the stirrups and hauled back on the reins with both hands, trying to help his horse gain good footing.

Suddenly a long hemp rope whistled through the air and dropped over the head of the sorrel and the voice of Mateo came from the shore where he sat on his big steeldust gelding, the rope dallied around his saddle horn, "Give him his head, let me pull him out. Hang on!" shouted Mateo. And Pete leaned back away from the rope, let the sorrel have his head and gave the slack to Mateo, who jerked his horse's head around and dug spurs to his ribs, prompting the big steeldust to dig deep and with the rope over his thigh, Mateo encouraged his mount to "Pull boy, pull!"

The sorrel quit fighting the quicksand, let the rope pull him away and Pete and the gelding, once free of the quicksand, found solid footing and climbed the bank. Pete breathed deep, leaned over to slip the rope off the neck of the sorrel, and stroked the gelding's neck, speaking softly to the faithful mount. He grinned when Mateo came alongside, shook his head, and said, "If I'da had a rifle handy, I'da shot that big bay! He's been trouble this whole drive an' I'm done with him!" he growled. He grinned, looked at Mateo and said, "Thanks! Wouldn'ta made it without'chu!"

"Anytime!" answered Mateo. That was the code of the men of the west. Do what you can to help who you can, and it'll come back to you sometime, somewhere down the line.

CHAPTER 28

ELK MOUNTAIN

With the North Platte and its quicksand behind them, another early start gave them a fresh new day as the sun bent long lances of gold over the eastern horizon to light the way. They crossed Pass Creek, took the road as it sided Rattlesnake Creek, but when the road and creek parted company, the trail bent northeast. Eli usually rode far ahead, serving as a second scout and hunter for fresh meat, but he also liked the solitude and took advantage of every opportunity to find a promontory to search the land about them for any sign of hostiles. Off his right shoulder the big black timbered Elk Mountain stood sentinel over the vast sagebrush plains. He chuckled as he sat atop a long mesa and thought, *Whoever named it Elk mountain musta been nippin' at the jug cuz that looks more like a sleeping buffalo!*

The shape of the mountain *was* that of a downed buffalo with its hump often whitened by winter's snow, but it was spring and most of the snow had long since made its getaway down the sluices of the many runoff creeks that creased the shoulders of the big mountain.

Eli sat atop a flat rock that lay in the shade of a solitary juniper standing alone on the flat crest of the long mesa. He had his binoculars in hand and scanned the flats, especially the Overland Trail that was their chosen route. He spotted what he thought was a hunting party of natives, a band of eight that was trailing three pack horses loaded with meat. They were moving north and would cross the road, but well before the herd came near. He was hopeful they would be long gone and not have any scouts out that would spot the herd, for he knew the horses would be a tempting prize for the native warriors.

He looked back along the road to see the rising cloud of dust from the herd, guessed it to be at least five miles away from the point of crossing for the hunting party. He wondered about where Charlie might be but was certain he would not be careless enough to be seen by the hunting party. Eli continued to watch and waited until the natives had crossed over and disappeared into the gullies and ravines that were thick with cottonwoods, willows and piñon. He slipped the binoculars back into the saddlebags and swung back aboard the big claybank, and with the grey close behind, returned to the notch he used to climb the mesa and dropped off onto the grassy flats.

The stage road bent around the lower end of Elk Mountain, covering land with rim rock buttes, sagebrush covered red dirt ridges, slopes marked with tilted moss covered sandstone holding stunted piñon and juniper bushes that dug roots into the smallest of crevices. Long dead twisted cedar showed grey trunks and skeletal branches that stood as sentinels over the hillsides. It was an amazing land and Eli grinned, shaking his head as he thought of the remarkable imagination of the Creator that stood upon nothing where there was no place to stand, and reached out into the emptiness of space to snatch something from nothing and hold it in his hands to mold and shape and create the marvelous handiwork that only He could form and appreciate. And He stood back, grinned, and said, "It is good!" Eli chuckled and spoke aloud, "It is good!"

Charlie was sitting in the shade of a lone ponderosa beside the road and grinned as Eli approached. He stood, nodded over his left shoulder, "Thought that'd be a good place to hold the herd for the night."

Eli glanced to the lowering sun, looked where Charlie pointed and saw the remains of an army fort. He looked at Charlie, "That Fort Halleck?"

"Used to be. It's been abandoned for a couple years now, but most of the stockade is still in place, many of the buildings have been taken, a dugout still shows, but..." he shrugged. They walked nearer and saw the big double gates standing open and askew. Some of the logs in the palisade were down, others missing, probably taken by some nearby farmer to use on his place.

Eli nodded, "Yeah, looks like it'll do, won't need so many men on guard through the night, they might get some much-needed rest." He turned to Charlie, "Did you see the hunting party?"

He grinned, nodded, "But they didn't see me!"

―――――

A FEW MILES out of Fort Halleck, they crossed the Medicine Bow river and east southeast on the Overland Trail. By the end of the second day out of Halleck, the long barracks and several of the officer quarters of Fort Sanders were seen. Sanders was a newer post and larger, with a parade ground in the middle and a tall flagpole holding the red, white and blue banner of the U.S. flying in the wind.

The grassy flats were inviting for the herd and the men wasted little time in getting the animals settled down. A big haystack that sat away from the fenced grounds of the fort, was also fenced and safe from the tired horses. A small creek nearby offered ample water and while the men were tending the herd, Eli went to the fort to meet the commandant.

As he entered the gate of the fort, he was stopped by a trooper, "What's your business?" he asked, standing with his rifle held across his chest as he scowled at the stranger.

"I'd like to see the commandant. I'm Lieutenant Colonel Elijah McCain and we're taking a herd of cavalry remounts east to General Sheridan."

The guard turned to another trooper and sent him on his way to tell the commandant of the visitor. Eli grinned, looked at the man, "What is the name of your commandant?"

"Captain Mizner of the 18th U.S. Infantry, sir." He dropped his eyes, and shook his head slightly, and spoke softly, "At least for now, he is."

Eli frowned, "Is he being replaced?"

"That's the scuttlebutt, sir. Has to do with the rail-road and such. Gotta a bunch o' high-ranking officers and important people comin' out here soon."

The other trooper came at a quick step and said, "The Captain will see you now, sir."

Eli nodded and nudged Rusty forward, the grey had been left behind with Jeremy at the cook wagon. He pulled up before the headquarters building, stepped down and looked around. It was a large post, recently built, well-kept and all the buildings were of log, but another one was being built and Eli recognized it as the powder house. He slapped the reins over the hitchrail and stepped up to enter the headquarters where he was greeted by a corporal seated behind a desk who said, "Go on in, sir. The Captain is waiting."

When Eli entered, the captain snapped a smart salute and asked, "Are you my replacement?"

Eli grinned, motioned for the captain to be seated, and seated himself. "No, captain, I just wanted to check in with you. We're taking a herd of remounts east to Fort Hays, General Sheridan, and wanted to know if you needed any for your men."

The captain relaxed, obviously relieved, "I was told I was being replaced, but not who would be taking my place. It has to do with the coming railroad, and General Grant wants General Dodge to engineer the railroad and, well, there's a bit of a conflict. However, they are platting a town just north of here and they expect the railroad to reach here soon.

"We did the work of building the fort, so, now someone else will take over and do the business of the army. I'm a builder, not a soldier."

"I see, well, you've done a fine job, captain. You're to be commended. And I take it by that, you won't be needing any remounts?"

He grinned, "Since this is the 18th Infantry, no, we won't be needing any remounts."

"Do you know where you'll be going?" asked Eli.

"Hopefully, back to Ohio, that's home for most of us and we're anxious to get there. Most of the others that mustered out after the war are already home, but we've, well, I think you know how it goes. For a while, I thought I'd be going east to build another fort a couple days east of here. The Union Pacific had declared it was

going to plat a town there for their western headquarters, and the army is building a fort. I think it'll be called
Fort Russell. But they brought in the 30th Infantry under
Colonel John Stevenson to build it, so..." he grinned and
shrugged.

"Yes, I know how it is with the army, and like any
other governmental organization, those that make the
plans, and the orders are the ones that really don't know
what they're doing, but they make the orders anyway.
Usually has something political about it. So, yes I know, I
do indeed. I served under Sheridan, but mustered out
after it was over, but haven't really been home. I left
home to go to West Point, then was sent west, back to
the war, and..." he shrugged. "Since then, I've been on a
long hunt, my boys went missing and I had to track them
down, but we're together now and hopefully, we'll
deliver this herd and make it home after that."

"Where's home?"

"Actually, my home is Maryland, but my wife's was
Kentucky and that's where the boys grew up and
consider home."

The captain nodded, stood and extended his hand,
"Then I'll not keep you, Colonel. May you have a safe
and uneventful journey and make it home as you will."

"Thanks captain, but the uneventful part has already
been quashed, so..." he shrugged, shook the captain's
hand and turned to leave.

———

THIS WAS the place where the two branches of the
Overland trail merged, or split, depending on the direction. Eli knew the original military route followed Lodgepole Creek east, but now with the railroad doing so

much planning and building, the route they preferred was more to the south and followed Lonetree creek and that was the route he preferred to take. The captain had explained the routes and suggested the southern route. "Until you get to Crow Creek Crossing, that's gonna be the new mountain region headquarters for the Union Pacific in Dakota Territory, and it's just north of there where they're building the new fort to protect the railroad. Now they're talkin' about making this here part of the country into Wyoming Territory. But after you get past all the railroad doin's, the road does meet up with Lodgepole Creek and you can follow that into the new state of Nebraska." He chuckled, "But I reckon you know all that, and I s'pose you also know the Lakota and others are not very happy 'bout all that, especially the railroad."

As Eli stepped through the door, the captain added, "And as the ol' mountain men used to say, 'Keep your topknot on!'" and chuckled as Eli moved through the doorway and waved over his shoulder.

CHAPTER 29

NEBRASKA

They moved southeast from Fort Sanders into wild country, more so than anything seen before. Ponderosa, fir, and a smattering of aspen struggled to shield the massive rocks from the stage road, but they stood tall and proud. Massive granite boulders tinted pink by feldspar and quartz with orange and grey lichen clamoring up from the bottom, they appeared to have been stacked by the ancients preparing for a monstrous rock fight. Boulders that would dwarf a Conestoga wagon and even the biggest building man could build beside them. All stacked atop one another as if set aside by the Creator readying to build a monument of stone. A few clearings pushed aside the pines, juniper, and sagebrush to offer a dining table of green grass and clear-water ponds and to entice the horses to refresh themselves.

After a mid-day break in the shadows of the big rocks, they bent a little more southward and took the road that sided Lone Tree Creek. Another day and a half on the well-traveled road beside Lone Tree Creek fighting the numerous freight wagons carrying supplies for the railroad crews and the cursing freighters and railroaders, they approached the edge of the rapidly growing town of Cheyenne. Named Crow Creek Crossing by the builders of the railroad, the citizens soon changed the name to Cheyenne, after the populous land of the natives.

"Jeremy, you go with Charlie and re-stock as you need, we'll keep the herd moving till we're past the settlement and away from all this," motioning to the dust cloud that trailed a group of loaded down freighters. "It'll prob'ly be dark when you get to camp. We'll have a cookfire goin' and if you'll leave the coffee makin's with the other wagon, we'll keep the drovers happy drinkin' java, at least until you get there an' can fix 'em somethin' more substantial."

"Yassuh, boss," grinned Jeremy, getting an elbow in his ribs from Missy. They both chuckled and Jeremy pulled the cook wagon beside the water wagon and handed off the big coffee pot, a bag of cups, some Arbuckles, and the stakes and cross bar for hanging the pot over the fire. He stood and waved to Eli and nodded to Charlie as they started for Cheyenne.

With the coffee pot rumbling and humming its prairie ballad, the men drifted into the camp beside the water wagon. With rolling hills to the south and north of them, the meandering Crow Creek beside them, they were camped in the basin of the Crow Creek that carried a vast stretch of tall grasses that gently waved in the cool evening air. The sun was lowering amidst a golden sky and the glow of sunset bathed the valley with a hint of gold that lay quietly on the grassy sea. As was their habit, they crossed Crow Creek before making camp and the horse herd lazed in the flats with full stomachs and although some stood hipshot, most had stretched out in the cool grass. They were content and were enjoying the rest when the creaking and rattling cook wagon rolled into camp, with a grinning Jeremy singing *Swing Low, Sweet Chariot, comin' for to carry me home*... His deep bass voice and Missy's melodic harmony brought smiles to all the drovers as they sat around the cookfire, nursing their coffee while they waited for Jeremy to fix their supper.

As the black of night began to lift its star sprinkled skirt to show the dusky blue of the coming day, grumpy men rolled from their blankets as Charlie and Eli sat beside the fire with steaming cups of coffee held with both hands, elbows on knees and they grinned at the antics of the drovers as they shook out their boots, pulled them on over holey socks, and wiped the sleep from their dust encrusted eyes. The men dispersed to the different clusters of kinnikinnick, chokecherry, and service berry bushes and soon returned for their morning feed.

Eli always kept his horses picketed near his bedroll and he left his perch on the fireside rock, tossed out the dregs of the coffee, and started for the horses. Rusty lifted his head, ears pricked, nostrils flaring as he snorted and stomped a foot. Eli glanced to the grey who stood beside the claybank and was alerted and looking the same direction. Before Eli could turn, he felt the rumble through the ground and turned around to see a monstrous cloud of dust that lifted and grew just a few miles from their camp. He turned to the hungry men and shouted, "Mount up! We got trouble comin'!"

Eli grabbed up the bit and bridle, apologized to Rusty, "Sorry boy, ain't got time to warm it up for ya'," slapped the saddle blanket on, swung the saddle over Rusty's back and reached for the cinch. Quickly strapping things down, he stepped into the stirrup, glanced to Grey who was wanting to come, but nodded his head, "You're stayin' here boy," and dug heels into the ribs of the stallion and headed for the herd. As the men came from the remuda, Eli directed them to different points of the herd, "That's a herd of buffalo comin', and the horses ain't gonna like it! We'll need to keep 'em circlin' to keep 'em from breakin' out and runnin' off!"

After the first two hours of the thundering herd of buffalo rolling over the hills, the horse herd began to settle down, most standing with heads high, watching the phenomena of the prairie, the rolling carpet of brown that shook the earth, bathed it with dust, and grumbled with every step. Orange coated calves romped beside grumpy mothers, brawny bulls herded their charge as they left behind a wide swath of churned grown with little green still showing. Eli sat astride Rusty, leaning on the saddle horn with arms crossed, and slowly shook his head as he glanced to Charlie Two Toes, "Now that's a sight that most don't get to see," grinning and enjoying the rarity.

Charlie grumbled, "And if the white man has his way, they will soon be gone."

Eli sat up, looked at Charlie, "Yeah, I've seen too many hunters kill everything they could see, leave the carcasses and take only the hides. Nothing can survive like that." What he did not say was what he was thinking about the whispered strategy of General Sherman who had voiced his opinion of the natives that the bison must be obliterated to control the tribes. Eli shook his head at the thought of such extreme measures, but he also knew that those in power such as Sherman and Grant would resort to anything and were limited by nothing, in their pursuit of absolute control.

The men ate in shifts, with six to eight always on the

herd. Although the horses had settled down, it was still an unnerving sight for both man and horse to have the entire horizon to be blanketed by the massive brown herd of bison. Jeremy and Missy had worked hard most of the day preparing a special supper for the men and as the last of the bison passed, the sun was lowering once again, the men stumbled into camp.

Tired, weary, and hungry after the long day in the saddle, the men stripped their horses, rubbed them down, led them to water and loosed them in the makeshift corral for the remuda. As they returned to the cookfire, dirty faces began to show grins, heads lifted and Mateo asked, "Is that apple pie I smell?"

"Sho nuff!" answered the squeaky voiced Missy, her grin splitting her face as she eyed all the men who had become family during the long drive.

"Whooooeeee!" declared John Swain, who had just returned to drover duty instead of driving the water wagon. "I ain't smelled nuthin' so sweet since I was in knee britches in muh momma's kitchen!"

"Like yo momma tol' you, you gots to clean yo plate o' you ain't gonna git none!" giggled the grinning Missy. "We made 'nuff fo' eve'body, but yo' ain't gittin' nuthin' less'n you do! An' yo' gots to wash yo plate after! The sink's right'chonder!" pointing to the willow shrouded Crow creek.

And on this night, both men and horses were sleeping with full stomachs and tired bodies, yet all were looking forward to the coming day and the soon end of the long drive.

The herd moved at a good pace, riding into the rising sun that threw long lances of gold into the sky, chasing the last vestiges of darkness to its retreat in the west. A cool breeze in their faces promised a good day of travel, the dust cloud of the thousand horses blown to the west, blanketing the green basin with a coat of powdery grey. The muddy remains of Crow Creek was behind them, and the tawny shades of bunch grass and gramma waved them onward to Muddy Creek, their chosen site for today's nooning.

CHAPTER 30

CHICKEN

E li was down on one knee, his hand moving through the grass as he looked at the retreating plains that stretched further than the eye could see, and a low rumbling booming sound sifted through the tall grasses causing Eli to grin at the memory of the mating call of the prairie chicken. He slowly stood, looking over the sea of bluestem and grama grasses to search for the male that was sounding his call as he looked for his mate, but the elusive bird of the prairie grasses was not to be seen. It was the afternoon of the third day since the passing of the bison herd, they had followed Lodgepole Creek into Nebraska and the stage road had become more of a supply route for the Union Pacific Railroad that was steadily pushing its way west, but the increased numbers of freighters and stagecoaches as well as the greater number of settlers and men coming to look for work on the railroad, was like moving against the tide of the rolling seas.

Eli stepped aboard Rusty, sat a moment to scan the

flats ahead. This land was deceiving, low rolling hills that appeared as if there is no cover, no change in terrain, no place to hide, but what looked like flats, more often had the low swales, dips that could hide a band of hundreds of Cheyenne, Arapaho, Kiowa or Lakota, all tribes that were fighting the onslaught of the tide of settlers. He also knew that there would be nothing as enticing and tempting for native warriors than this great herd of horses. In the distance, he saw movement, and he leaned back to slip the binoculars from the case in his saddle-bags. Turning back, he brought the glasses to his eyes and spotted a lone rider coming toward him at a lope. It was Charlie Two Toes, but as he watched, there was no waving, no apparent signal of impending danger, but Charlie was one that did not push his horse, especially on a hot spring day such as this, unless he had a purpose.

Eli scanned the land around, searching for any sign of danger, but seeing nothing amiss, he cased the binoculars and stepped down to await the scout. Charlie reined up, stepped down beside Eli, "Been seein' quite a bit o' sign of raiding parties and more. Back yonder a ways, there was a camp, big 'un, I'm guessin' Cheyenne, but I saw some sign, broken arrow shaft, fletching and point, that coulda been Arapaho. I hear they been gettin' together and if so, they'd put a whole big bunch o' warriors on the warpath together."

"How big a bunch?"

"Oh, four, five hundred."

Eli frowned, looked directly at Charlie, "Five hundred?"

Charlie just nodded, shaking his head and getting that far-off look in his eyes as he gazed across the grassy flats. "Talked to a fella back in Cheyenne town, said he heard they was workin' up for a big fight. All of 'em are riled up about the so'jer boys an' settlers not keepin' the treaty and the bigwigs keep stealin' their huntin' lands for them settlers. There's been a lot o' fightin' down Colorado way, along the South Platte, been takin' women an' children captive to replace what they lost, like in Sand Creek, killin' the men and burnin' the homes, wagons, an' more. He said it ain't pretty. An' you know what any of 'em would do for a herd like this'n."

"You think we need to have somebody on our backtrail?"

"Wouldn't hurt. Ain't none of 'em gonna come on us straight on, they'd like to come up behind us, unknown, drive the herd right over us an' take 'em all."

"You still thinkin' we'll follow the Lodgepole down into Colorado - Julesburg - to get supplies - then turn east?"

"Yeah, been through this country lotsa times, plenty of water. Now, around Julesburg, there's more hills, but we'll cross back into Nebraska some'eres thereabouts, and it stays hilly, but there's lotsa creeks. But we'll prob'ly follow Spring Creek or Red Willow Creek south to the Republican River, cross it and then there's Beaver Creek, Sappa Creek, and Prairie Dog Creek. Then we'll cross North Fork of the Solomon, the South Fork of the Solomon, then we hit the Saline." He paused, chuckling, "An' we follow that all the way to Fort Hays!"

"So, whaddya figger? Timewise, I mean?"

"Oh, week, week an' a half, give or take, you know," chuckled Charlie, shaking his head and stubbing his toe in the dirt.

"Yeah, an' with the extra threat of three or four tribes

of restless and horse-hungry natives..." shrugged Eli. He walked back to the grey pack-horse and withdrew the Colt revolving shotgun, grabbed a handful of buckshot shells and grinned at Charlie, "I'm goin' huntin' some prairie chicken!"

"Lemme see that," asked Charlie, frowning at the unusual weapon. "Ain't never seen one like this," he said as he accepted the shotgun and began looking it over."

"Betcha I can get just as many with my Henry as you can with this," suggested Charlie, grinning.

"Maybe, but will there be anything left to eat after you do?"

"Then, let's just see what we can do, I'm gettin' hungry for fried chicken!"

The road they followed was south of the Lodgepole Creek and as the men mounted up for their competitive hunt, they started across the short distance to the tree lined creek. The prairie chicken would not be too far from water and the berry shrubs that grew near the wetlands of the Sandhills. Although not a water bird, the grouse and prairie chicken prefer the tall grasses nearby using those areas for their breeding sites. The two men reined up, stepped down and ground tied their horses and moved apart to flush out the well-hidden birds that had grown quiet with the sounds of predators approaching.

Within moments, a small covey took flight and Eli was quick to drop two but as he walked to retrieve the bounty, he heard Charlie cut loose with three rapid-fire shots from his Henry only to see him retrieve three headless chickens. Eli shook his head, grinned and had his attention taken by the fluttering sounds of birds taking flight. He turned to see another covey and quickly took aim and fired to drop another pair. He chuckled as he called out the Charlie, "If you got three, I've got four, so we might need at least a couple more!"

The words had no sooner fallen to the grass when the Henry barked again, and Charlie dropped another pair. Eli answered with another blast of his Colt shotgun and feathers drifted slowly to the ground. "That oughta do!" called Eli and the men came together by the horses and loaded their bounty into a flour sack carried in the pannier on Grey. Eli looked at Charlie, "I'll take these back to Jeremy and you can make another circle 'round those hills," nodding to the southeast, "'fore we leave these flats."

When Eli came alongside the cook wagon, he was greeted by a grinning Jeremy and Missy when Jeremy asked, "Whatchu got fer us, Boss?"

Eli shook his head, grinned and asked, "How 'bout some fried chicken, taters an' gravy an' biscuits for supper tonight?" and tossed the big bag of feathered bounty up to the man.

"You got us some chicken? Howsomever'd you do that? Raid some farmer's henhouse?"

Eli chuckled, "Nope, God just smiled down on me an' said, 'Go fetch' so I did!" He chuckled again, "Haven't you ever heard of prairie chicken?"

"Wal, I'll be hornswaggled, if'n that don' beat all." He lifted his eyes from the bag and grinned at Eli, "Fried chicken it is!"

———

AS THEY BROKE camp in the wee hours of the early morning, old sol had yet to show his face, but when Missy had found a batch of duck eggs in a marsh near the creek, the men had their fill of eggs and bacon for breakfast, using the last of the pork belly for their bacon. The men were content, bellies filled, and the horses had a good nights graze with cold fresh water, and all were eager to be back on the trail.

Eli chose to be the first to take the scout of their back-trail and watched as the men pushed the herd onto the trail to follow the southward bend of the Lodgepole Creek. They would cross the South Platte River before their mid-day break and Jeremy had left biscuits and the rest of the fried chicken with the water wagon while he and Missy, together with Jubal and Joshua, went into Julesburg to resupply, hopefully it would be the last time before reaching Fort Hays.

As he stepped aboard Rusty, he stood in his stirrups and shading his eyes from the growing light, he searched for high ground to make his first survey of the area, especially their back-trail, to see if they were being shadowed by any of the natives. His choices were few, but he spotted a flat topped butte and started to the south west to use that as his promontory. When he neared the bluff, he spotted what appeared to be a trail that split the rimrock and offered a route to the top. Within moments he was atop the butte and stepped down, rifle and binoculars in hand. A long-dead twisted cedar offered a seat, but he had to evict a skinny lizard and a scorpion before he settled down, he lifted the glasses and began his scan. After several moments, the only life he saw was a trio of deer, one buck and two doe, a distant herd of pronghorn antelope, two coyotes, but nothing with only two legs. He made one more scan and caught his breath as Rusty jerked his head up, looking back to the trail they used to mount the butte. His ears were pricked, and he stomped a hoof, snorted, and Eli turned. Six painted-for-war Cheyenne Dog Soldier warriors were fanned out before him, all holding weapons from rifles to bows and lances and war clubs. One man with a feathered headpiece that bristled in the breeze, scowled and growled, "You have horses - we take!" but he motioned in the direction of his horse herd, not just the two that stood beside him.

CHAPTER 31

FLIGHT

Eli was standing between Rusty and Grey and rested his hand on the stock of his Winchester that sat in the scabbard and mostly out of sight of the warriors. He spoke in a soft tone that only the horses could hear, and he knew Rusty had an uncanny way of understanding what Eli said, or seemed to, and now he spoke to both horses, "When I slap your rumps, charge through that bunch and take out as many as you can, then go back to the herd so they'll know what happened."

Eli lifted his eyes to the leader of the Dog Soldiers and with a sudden shout, he slapped the horses as he slipped the Winchester from the scabbard, shouted, "Now! Go boys!" The horses lunged forward as if joined at the hip, charging into the semi-circle of warriors that were taken completely by surprise as they scrambled to get out of the way. Rusty grabbed at one by his right shoulder with his teeth, ripping a chunk of flesh from the warrior's shoulder, and twisted in the middle and kicked at another, the shod hooves taking the warrior in the head and shoulder with a resounding thud that did little to mask the cracking of bones as the warrior's jaw was broken and knocked askew and his shoulder crackled under the impact.

Grey struck out in much the same way, stretching his head out to sink his teeth into the back of the neck of one man, kicking out as he went past another to break the rifle-holding arm of another. Grey was close behind Rusty as they took the break in the rimrock and slid down the steep trail, hind hooves sliding in the loose soil, their rumps dragging in the dirt behind. In that instant, they were gone - tails flying high as they took to the flats after the herd.

Eli jacked a round into the chamber of his yellow-boy and waded into the melee, firing with his rifle at his hip. Two warriors clamored to their feet, grabbing at their weapons, but the .44 slugs from the Winchester drove them both back to the ground. Eli turned, looking at the downed warriors, two were dead, four on the ground, bleeding. He was tempted to give the coup-d'état, but it was not his way to kill a defenseless man, even if he was the enemy that was more than willing to kill him. He stepped before the one who had spoken and scowled, "You're not getting any of our horses. Those are for the soldiers at Fort Hays!"

The warrior struggled to speak, but with his jaw flopping and blood flowing, he could only grunt. Eli looked at the others, glancing from one to the other, and started to the rim of the butte. Now afoot, he needed a horse, and he searched the trees below for the horses of the Dog Soldiers, spotted them, and with a last glance to the downed and moaning warriors, he shook his head and started down the steep trail, slipping and sliding, to get to the horses. He picked out a strong looking blue roan, grabbed up his lead and with a handful of mane, swung aboard. He thought about taking the other horses, but decided against it, thinking they would not be worth the trouble, and slapped legs to his mount and headed out after the herd.

———

TALL BULL, leader of the *Masikota* band of the Cheyenne people, the band that was Dog Soldiers, stood before the council in the big lodge. The muscles of his chest and upper arms rippled in the firelight as he glowered at those seated around the center fire, the silver arm band reflected the light, a hairpipe bone breast plate lifted with every breath, his feathered headdress moved with the slightest breeze, his look was intimidating as he glanced around the circle of warrior leaders. He was a respected leader and warrior, even though he was of mixed blood, both Cheyenne and Lakota, he also had a reputation of treachery, even against his own people. He had walked the path of Porcupine Bear, the founder of the Dog Soldiers who had been expelled from the Dog Soldiers after killing one of their own. Before him sat his sub-chief, White Horse, and other leaders, of the *Oivimana*, War Bonnet, Yellow Hand, leader of the *Hevhaitaniu* and his fellow chief, Big Man. White Antelope, the leader of the *Hisiometanio*, sat alone at the edge of the group. Tall Bull began, "We decided to join with Red Cloud of the *Oglala* and if we come to them with the great herd of the white men, we will be a mighty force and will kill many white men!"

Yellow Hand and Big Man nodded their agreement,

but White Antelope asked, "How do you plan to get this great herd? Do you not know the Buffalo Soldiers have been moving in our lands and would fight for those horses? Did not the white man that killed our warriors say those horses are for the soldiers at Fort Hays?"

Many of the others mumbled their concern, slapping the ground beside them and nodding their agreement with White Antelope.

Tall Bull answered, "Is White Antelope afraid of the Buffalo Soldiers? Will you not ride with us against the white eyes and the Buffalo soldiers? We have never seen a herd the size of that which moves across our lands, it is a sign from the Great Spirit that he has brought before us, a great gift, and you will not accept that gift from the Great Spirit? Could it not be that Sweet Medicine has brought them before us as he brought the *Maahótse*, our Sacred Arrows?"

Yellow Hand asked, "Who will lead this band of warriors against the whites to take the great horse herd?"

Tall Bull stood tall, a smug look painting his rugged face, "I will lead them! I know Sweet Medicine would have us take the herd for our fight against the many whites that come into our lands and kill our buffalo!" The warriors in the council slapped their hands against the ground and sounded their war cries, looking at one another and showing their fiercest face, anticipating a great fight and victory with the prize being a thousand horses to carry their people in the war against the white men.

————

"SOUNDS like you had yourself some excitement!" declared Charlie, reaching for the coffeepot.

"More'n I wanted, that's for sure," answered Eli. "But I did find out that the Cheyenne, namely the Dog Soldiers, are on our trail."

"Any idea as to the number?" asked Charlie.

Eli shook his head, "No way of knowin'. There were only six in the bunch that came after me."

"So, whaddaya reckon we should be doin'?"

"We'll keep movin', keep a watch on our back trail and if they get any closer, well I reckon we might hafta travel at night."

After Eli's encounter, they made long days of the drive, crossing the Republican River, Beaver Creek, Sappa Creek, Prairie Dog Creek and both forks of the Solomon, none of which were much of a crossing, and always had at least two men on watch for their backtrail. After two more days, they were alarmed when Mateo came riding up at a full gallop, waving his sombrero overhead. When he slid his mount to a stop between them, Eli glanced to Charlie, then to Mateo, frowned and asked, "What is it, Mateo?"

"The Cheyenne, looks to be a hundred of 'em, maybe more."

"How close?"

"I was hanging back about 10 miles, saw with your binoculars, so..." he shrugged.

Eli lifted his head to the sky, looked about, "I think we'll have enough light tonight to keep movin' a spell. We go as far as we think the horses'll do, then make camp but with double the guards out."

"Sounds reasonable," chuckled Charlie.

The drovers began drifting into the camp, hungry eyes looking to Jeremy and Missy, hopeful of some more of Missy's pies or other sweets, but this night's supper would be just the basics with antelope steaks, potatoes, biscuits and gravy, with plenty of hot stiff coffee. As the crew was finishing their supper, Eli stepped closer and explained, "We've got Cheyenne Dog Soldiers on our backtrail, and we'll be moving out after dusk. We'll be travelin' by moonlight, and we'll need to move as quietly as possible, no shoutin' and such. We're hopin' to make the Saline River, cross over, and if we hafta make a stand, we'll do it on the far side, catch 'em crossin' the river. So, go ahead and relieve the others and after they have their supper, we'll be movin' out."

The moon was waxing full, while the few clouds showed shadows in the dark sky. The early stars had lit their lanterns and seemed to dance in the darkness. When Eli gave the signal with a one note shrill whistle, the drovers crowded close to the herd and started them moving. They let the horses take their own gait and the herd moved at a fast walk, but after the first few miles, they settled into an easy walk. The greatest problem for the drovers was to stay awake in the rocking saddles. Few sounds came from the horses, unlike a herd of cattle where there are always the complaining bellows of many, the horses moved more quietly than Eli hoped. The dust made the drovers slip their scarves over their faces, and the creak of saddle leather, the jingle of spurs and the groaning of wagon wheels blended into a lullaby that encouraged the drovers to lapse into a half-awake mood.

Eli was with Charlie as they scouted ahead, charging Mateo with the rear guard to sound any warning of approaching Dog Soldiers. They saw the long line of cottonwoods that sided the Saline River, standing as dark ogres lining the bank, replacing the long line of the flat horizon with the irregular shadows of the tall trees. Eli frowned, looked at Charlie, "Do you hear that?"

Charlie reined up beside Eli, frowning and cocking his head to one side, "Yeah, sounds like singin', but who'd be singing out here?"

CHAPTER 32

10TH

The strains of the song drifted across the rippling waters of the Saline River, moonbeams bouncing across the ripples in time with the music. Deep voices let the song roll through the night and drift onto the plains. A concertina, a mouth harp, and the voice of a gently played fiddle wrapped the words in a somber, melancholy tune that sounded like the old minstrel song of Camptown Races, but it rolled slowly across the flats. A smattering of campfires on the far bank of the river told of the presence of men.

> *We're fighting bulls of the Buffaloes,*
> *Git a goin' -- git a goin'*
> *From Kansas' plains we'll hunt our foes;*
> *A trottin' down the line.*
> *Our range spreads west to Santa Fe,*
> *Git a goin' -- git a goin'.*
> *From Dakota down the Mexican way;*
> *A trottin' down the line.*

Goin' to drill all day
Goin' to drill all night,
We got our money on the buffaloes,
Somebody bet on the fight.
Pick up your saddle and make it light.
Git a rollin' -- git a rollin'.
You are training fast for a hard fight;
A rollin' down the line.

"Halt! Who goes there?" came a shout from the shadows, stopping Eli and Charlie.

"We're friendlies!" answered Eli. "I'm Colonel Elijah McCain comin' with a herd of horses for General Sheridan at Fort Hays!"

"Hold!" The guard lowered his voice and spoke to the other guard, "You watch 'em, I'll get the Captain," and trotted off into the trees.

Within moments the guard returned, two other men following close behind. They stopped at the edge of the trees, their presence unseen due to the deep shadows of the darkening night. Several clouds had rolled in and dimmed even the pale light of the blue moon hanging high overhead.

"Who goes there?" came a raspy question from the shadows.

"Colonel Elijah McCain with a herd of horses for General Sheridan at Fort Hays!" answered Eli.

"C'mon across!" rang the answer.

Eli and Charlie nudged their mounts down the bank and into the water of the Saline River. It was a low-water river with gravelly bottom and not enough water to reach the stirrups on their saddles, but the horses dipped their noses and took a drink without hesitating a step. As they climbed the low bank on the far side, two uniformed men stepped from the shadows and Eli recognized the uniform of one as that of a captain. "Evenin' captain, are you the officer in charge?"

The man stepped forward, extending his hand as Eli stepped down, "That I am, sir, I'm Captain George Armes, and you say you are Colonel McCain?"

"Lieutenant Colonel, retired, I served with General Sheridan in '64 and '65."

The two men shook hands and typically sized one another up with a quick up and down glance. The captain stood close to six feet, broad shouldered, a grin that split his van dyke moustache and beard that was shot with grey, and steely grey eyes. While most officers left their sabers in their camp, his still dangled from his belt and he rested his left hand on the hilt as he looked at Eli.

"You say you have a herd of horses for Fort Hays?" he asked, leaning to look past Eli, searching the dim lighted flats for the herd.

"That's right. They'll be along shortly, along with about a hundred Cheyenne Dog Soldiers that would like to steal 'em."

"Dog Soldiers? Are you sure?"

"I am, had a run-in with a few of 'em a couple days back and they let it be known, they wanted our horses. I disagreed and left a few of 'em dead and dying."

"Well, you've played hob! And I've only a company of men, and they're all coloreds!"

Eli frowned, "Buffalo soldiers? Can't ask for better! And if you've got a full company…"

A first sergeant had stood silently beside the captain until Eli spoke and he stepped forward, saluted, "Company F, 10th Cavalry, Sir! Battle tested and ready, Sir!"

"As you were sergeant!" ordered the captain. He turned to face Eli, "We *have* fought in a few skirmishes under General Sherman, his winter campaign against the Cheyenne, Arapaho, and Comanche. They have always proved themselves capable." He paused, looked from the sergeant to Eli, "What would you recommend sir?"

Eli turned to Charlie, "Charlie, you tell the men to take the herd across up that way a little, don't wanna run over the camp of the cavalry." He paused as Charlie reined his mount around and splashed across the river, turned to the captain, "I think it'd be best to line your men out on this side of the river, there's good cover and they would have a good field of fire as the attackers hit the water. Don't you think so, captain?"

"Yes, yes I do. I agree, sir." He paused, turned to the sergeant, "Deploy the men, sergeant, and get the howitzer around so we can use it also!"

"You have a howitzer?" asked an incredulous Eli.

"We have an M1841 Mountain Howitzer, 12 pounder."

"That'll make 'em sit up and take notice!" declared a grinning Eli, turning to look through the trees to the encampment of the 10th, watching as the men were disbursed to different firing positions and saw the team of mules pulling the howitzer into place.

The rumble of the herd turned Eli back to face the river and the far bank to see the shadowy dust cloud that trailed the herd. They were coming at a faster pace than before, and he assumed Mateo had made them pick up the pace with a report of the approaching Cheyenne. Charlie sat his mount near the river bank and stood in his stirrups, motioning to the drovers where they were to cross. The massive herd crashed through the underbrush and cottonwoods, driving into the water and splashing across, the point riders waiting on the far side and drove the leaders of the herd upstream and made them swing away from the trees to start circling and settle down. Within moments, the entire herd had crossed, and the drovers were keeping the herd circling until they settled down. Jeremy and the cook wagon and the water wagon had drawn aside to let the herd pass and now pulled up at the edge of the trees to start making camp. He knew the tired men would be wanting coffee and could be tempted with the bear sign donuts made by Missy.

The Cheyenne had followed and were a short distance behind, but the entire herd crossed before they showed themselves. With the flats of the prairie holding the only cover in the form of scraggly sage and cholla cactus, the warriors pulled up short and rallied around their chiefs. Within moments, they spread out and sent the first wave of attackers on the charge. They were quickly answered by the deep-throated howitzer that parted the charging warriors and silenced many of the war cries. When the smoke cleared, several horses lay dead and the scattered bodies of warriors littered the ground around the crater of the blast.

The second wave charged, but split to both sides, trying to avoid the howitzer's field of fire. As they neared the river, the fusillade of Spencer rifles roared and gunsmoke filled the cottonwoods and the front-line warriors felt the blast as .52 caliber lead balls ripped through the cottonwoods to unseat many of the charging, screaming Dog Soldiers. The surviving warriors quickly jerked their horses around and retreated to gather with their chiefs, just out of effective range of the Spencer rifles. But they did not reckon on the longer range of the mountain howitzer and when the big gun bucked, roared and spat the 12 pound explosive projectile that landed a mite short of the gathered leaders, but near enough to drive them further back.

Not to be dissuaded, Tall Bull lifted his war lance high overhead and screamed his war cry to send another onslaught of his warriors into the fray. The warriors lined out in a ragged line parallel to the riverbank, and at the given signal, they too screamed their war cries that greeted the slow rising morning sun, and charged into the guns of the Buffalo Soldiers, with Eli and many of the drovers beside them, only to be stopped by another fusillade that wilted their charge and sated their spirits. But Tall Bull was a smarter tactician than first believed. He had separated two groups of ten or more warriors and sent them up and downstream to flank the soldiers. When the second offensive stalled, the two war parties rose from the willows and underbrush at the edge of the tall cottonwoods and swarmed over the soldiers from behind. Screams of war cries clashed with the startled screams of surprised soldiers, but the proven men valiantly fought. When two mounted warriors charged the middle of the line, Eli and Charlie turned and fired from the hip, both taking the same warrior, their bullets driving him end over end off the back of his charging horse. The second warrior met the butt of a Spencer rifle swung like a bat by the hands of First Sergeant Tibbs who growled his own war cry, "You bunch o' cowards! Come at us from behind will ya!" as the heavy stock of the Spencer crashed into the skull of the screaming Dog Soldier who would never utter his war cry again. Within moments, the surprised Buffalo Soldiers had turned the tide of the battle by killing almost all of the flanking war parties, but a few did drive through the lines to make their escape across the river.

It was a discouraged and defeated war party that turned their backs on the Saline River and the valiant 10th Cavalry of Buffalo Soldiers. It was a humiliating defeat of the proud Tall Bull, but it would not prevent him from continuing his fight against the dreaded white settlers and their armies.

Eli sought out captain Armes and approached with his hand extended, "Good job, captain! Your men certainly proved themselves again! You should be proud of them!"

"They only did what they were trained to do, Colonel. After all, you can't expect much more from the coloreds, now, can you?"

Eli frowned, looked around at several of the nearby men who had undoubtedly heard the captain's remarks and he shook his head as he looked at the captain, "I would be proud to serve with these men. They have proven themselves worthy of any battle and I would never hesitate to fight alongside them!" He had lifted his voice so most of the men could hear his words of praise, then glanced at the captain who had a snarl painted on his face, but Eli shook his head and turned away. He had served with his kind before and was determined to never again be saddled with such contemptuous types.

CHAPTER 33

FORT HAYS

The lowering sun was warm on their backs as they drove the herd the last mile to Fort Hays. It was late on the second day after the skirmish with the Cheyenne and the post was a welcome sight. The fort was on a slight rise that afforded them a view of the surrounding plains, flat land everywhere. With no perimeter walls or fortification, the buildings of the fort, with the exception of the two-story stone blockhouse, looked more like a settlement than a military installation. Captain Armes rode beside Eli, Charlie was well ahead, and the twins rode point behind Eli and the captain. The ever-present dust cloud trailed the herd, readily marking their location and as usual, forcing the drovers to ride with scarves covering their faces, but nothing could keep the dust from their eyes as each man was often seen splashing water from their canteens on their dusty faces.

"The north side of the fort has ample graze, and the general has had us building fence around the field in anticipation of the arrival of this herd," explained the captain. "So, you'll need to take 'em below the rise on the back side."

"We can do that. My boys and I will be taking the first train east from here, they have young ladies waiting for them and they're anxious to get together, but the rest of the men will be staying around a few days. There is a depot in Hays City isn't there?"

"There is, but I'm sure General Sheridan would like to speak to you before you leave."

"Oh, I intend to see him, after all, he's responsible for us making this trip and I'll be looking to him for payment," chuckled Eli.

As they neared the fort, Eli's eyes were drawn to the stone blockhouse that stood tall on the highest point of the slight rise. It was easily identifiable as the only defensive structure of the entire fort, but it would be easily defended with the two story section in the middle rising high above the rest. A single story wing on either side allowed for additional rifle ports and windows with good fields of fire if needed. Nearby were the two story clapboard sided frame barracks, three barracks stretched out in a line that bordered the central parade ground. On the far side the officer's quarters and headquarters building of the same construction, stood sentinel over the parade ground and the towering flag-pole that proudly flew the stars and stripes. There were other buildings in various stages of construction and Eli grinned, thinking that one of them must be the ever-present and needful guardhouse.

Eli waved off as the boys led the herd to the back side of the post, following the lead of their scout, Charlie Two Toes. Eli looked to the captain, "Where's the telegraph office?"

Captain Armes pointed to the row of barracks and a

single story building beside them, "At the sutler's building, it's a temporary location until we get another built near the headquarters."

"The boys are expecting to find a telegram from their ladies and are anxious to find out it they made it to Louisville." Eli twisted around in his saddle, saw the cook wagon and water wagon break away from the herd and appeared to be following him. He reined up and waited for Jeremy to come near and when Jeremy stopped the wagon beside him, Eli offered, "You can pull your wagon over yonder between the barracks, near the sutlers and if you need anything from the sutler, just tell him to start a tally and I'll settle up soon's I get the payoff from the general. Oh, and my boys and I are taking the train from here and it'll be about a three day trip for us. If you and Missy could put together some food for us, I'll be over with the packs, and you can fill up a parfleche for us."

"Ya'll gonna be over for supper tonight?" asked Missy, showing her usual broad smile with her mischief filled eyes gleaming.

"Yes'm, we will. I'm sure we won't get a train until tomorrow sometime. And we'll be paying everyone tonight, and that includes the two of you!"

"I'se likin' the sound o' that, yessuh!" declared a grinning Jeremy.

Eli grinned, nodded, "Then we'll see you at suppertime."

———

"IT'S BEEN a long time since we were at Appomattox Court House," declared a grinning Sheridan as he stood behind his desk, extending his right hand to Eli.

"Yessir, it has been some time," answered Eli. The general waved him to a chair and both men were seated.

"I honestly did not think you'd make it all this way from California with a herd that size. Any problems?"

"Oh, nothing much, didn't really have any run-in with natives until we were almost here. A bunch of Cheyenne Dog Soldiers thought they would take the herd from us, but your boys of the 10th convinced them otherwise."

"Good men, those boys of the 10th. Wish I had 'em durin' the war," chuckled the general, as he reached to open the drawer of his desk, "I guess you're lookin' to get paid, aren't you?"

Eli grinned, chuckled, "Not just me. I've got some mighty good men, gauchos, vaqueros, and some colored cowboys that made the drive and they're thirsty, tired, dirty, and looking to clean-up, rest-up and get back home."

"So, what's the tally?"

Eli pulled out a paper from his shirt pocket, unfolded it and looked at the number, "One thousand, one hundred twenty-four at $60 equals $67,440. And if you could, I need about $3000 in cash, preferably gold coin. I need to pay-off the men."

"Alright, I'll make this draft for $64,440 and I'll need you to sign a receipt for $3000." He nodded to Captain Armes, "Captain, if you would take this," he handed the captain a slip of paper, "voucher to the paymaster, he should be able to give you the coin needed." The general finished making out the bank draft for the agreed amount and blew on it to dry the ink, then handed it to Eli. "And that comes with my thanks. Those horses are definitely needed. We have the 7th Cavalry under Colonel Custer coming in anytime now and we will need remounts for them and more."

The general grew stoic as he looked at Eli, "Didn't you serve at Fort Laramie before the war?"

"Yessir, I did."

"Did you meet any of the native chiefs, like Red Cloud and others?"

"I did,"

"Hmmm, we could use you as a scout, if you're interested. Same rank and pay, but you'd be a civilian scout. We have two good men, but their acquaintance with the natives is a little limited. Bill Hickok and Bill Cody, both good men, but I need somebody that knows both the cavalry and the natives. Interested?"

Eli dropped his eyes, chuckled, "You know, General, I've wondered just what I might get into after this drive, now that I've found my boys and they're returning to the home place, but one thing I never thought about was scouting. I have a good man with us that is a good scout, he's Pawnee, Charlie Two Toes, and if I was to do it, I'd like to bring him with me."

"We can do that, I'm sure he would be an asset."

"He would, but I'd need to talk to him first, and I'd need some time to think about it, but I will admit, it does sound tempting. After being in the mountains, I can't see myself returning to the flat lands."

"Well, the offer stands, I'd like to have you, what with your cavalry experience and your time with the natives, you know the language of any of 'em?" added the general as an afterthought.

"I know the sign language they use, and I know a little of the language of the Lakota," answered Eli. "I'll leave you a way to reach me by telegram, we'll be at the horse ranch of my wife's family in Louisville, Kentucky, at least until after I get the boys married off, then..." he shrugged.

The captain returned toting a leather satchel that jingled with every step. The bag contained the $3000 in gold coin and he handed it to the general who pushed a paper toward Eli, "Now you need to sign the receipt."

Eli grinned, "Can I trust you or do I need to count it?" he asked, looking sideways at the general and glancing to the captain.

"If you can trust me with your life like you did a couple times, surely you can trust me with your money," replied a grinning general Sheridan.

————

THE MEN WERE quick to finish their supper and to line up for their pay and each one was surprised and pleased when Eli said, "Men, like I promised, there will be a bonus since we lost so few horses. It's been a good drive and I'm proud to have ridden with you. So, in addition to the one hundred dollars promised, I've doubled it! Each man gets two hundred dollars and I have the gold coin for you right here," as he hefted the heavy leather pouch. "We'll need you to sign or make your mark in the ledger here," nodding toward the barrel top where the ledger rested in front of Joshua, "to show you've been paid, then you're on your own. The boys and I are taking the train east to Kentucky and the train runs both ways, so if you want to head back west, you can get a ticket as far as Cheyenne, Wyoming and maybe hook up with some freighters going west from there, or just point your horse west and ride 'er home!" Eli chuckled as he spoke, and his remark elicited chatter and laughter from the men.

As each man was paid, they shook hands with Eli and the boys and expressed their thanks to each one as did Eli when he greeted each man individually. It had been a good drive and they lost few horses, and none of the men were lost even through all the trials and the almost two thousand miles of the drive. Eli later said he considered it a miracle they could make the drive and he encouraged the boys to do as he would and offer their thanks to the Lord for His mercy.

CHAPTER 34

TRAIN

"So, how much extra will it cost us for a stock car for the horses?" asked Eli, his frustration with the ticket agent beginning to show.

"Well, sir, we hafta add on that car here, an' it'll go through to St. Louis, then they'll hafta be unloaded, taken across the river on the ferry, which you will also have to do, then get a stock car east bound goin' to Louisville. That's a heap'a doin' and the way they do it, it'll cost you most as much to take the horses as its gonna cost you your tickets."

"Then tally it up, we're not leavin' the horses."

"An' how many horses you takin'?"

"What difference does it make, they'll all be in the same car?"

"Wal, like I said, we be chargin' per horse."

"Four horses," groaned Eli, shaking his head.

When the agent tallied everything together, Eli pushed three stacks of 10 $20 gold pieces across the counter and received one $10 coin in change. He shook his head as he accepted the printed out tickets and handed them off to the boys. "Let's get the horses loaded," then turned to Joshua, "You have the parfleche of our food from Jeremy?"

"I do Pa, it's right here," he pointed to the end of a long bench where their satchels and bedrolls with their rifles and more lay waiting.

As they walked from the station Eli asked, "So, what did the girls have to say?"

"Oh, just that they're *all* excited to see us!" chuckled Joshua, looking sidelong at his Pa and grinning.

"What's that for?" asked Eli.

"The way we figger it, Pa, their ma is just as excited to see you as they are to see us!"

Eli stopped stock still, turned to look at the boys, "Whaddya mean by that?"

Jubal chuckled, "We're thinkin' she's got the same idea about you as the girls have about us!"

Eli started walking again, shaking his head and mumbling to himself, lifted his head to look at the grinning boys, "There ain't no way on God's green earth that I'm interested in that woman! I don't care how much money she has! Besides, I've been offered a job by General Sheridan that is beginning to look much more enticing than getting hitched!"

"What kind of job did the general offer you?" asked Joshua, frowning at his father.

"Scouting for the troopers fighting the Indians."

"And you think having every native on the great plains shooting at you would be preferable to marrying a good looking rich woman?"

"Well, that's one way of looking at it, I suppose," drawled Eli, grinning at the boys.

After getting the horses loaded, they packed their gear to the pullman car and took their places in the berth

assigned. With a parfleche full of food prepared by
Jeremy and Missy, who promised a good batch of bear
sign, they were ready for the journey. With a stop in St.
Louis to take the ferry across the river, then the rest of
the way to Louisville, it would be at least a three day trip
and temptation might get the best of them and the bear
sign might not last.

But the rations provided were more than sufficient
and the trip seemed to be one extensive feast enjoyed by
all. When the conductor walked through the cars
announcing, "Louisville, Louisville, Kentucky, next stop!"
they quickly stacked their bags and gear on the end of
the seat and looked out the windows to see the passing
buildings and hub-bub of the city. As the train drew near
the station, the imposing stone block structure made
them think more of a European castle or some state
capitol rather than a train station. With square pillars on
each corner that towered four stories high and the rest of
the structure three or three and a half stories, it was an
imposing structure, especially after crossing the wild
west where even an Indian tipi was considered
impressive.

It was nearing sunset when the train blew its whistle, and the steam was discharged as the wheels slowed
on the tracks. The lowering sun was painting the
station stone with shades of orange and people
crowded the platform beside the station. Jubal called
out, "There they are!" pointing at the window and the
three ladies, all with parasols and bonnets, each with a
pastel shade of cascading dress, decorated with lots of
lace and with reticules to match. They were a very
attractive trio and all sported broad smiles. Beside them
stood their Aunt Patience and her husband, their Uncle
Ephraim. As soon as they stepped to the exit, the girls

called out in voices that sounded almost like screams, "There they are!" and lifted their skirts and hurried closer. Warm embraces were had with the two couples and Geneviève offered a coy smile to Eli, but he ducked his head and fidgeted with their gear to unload it from the steps.

Ephraim came near, "Here, let me help you with that," he offered, and Eli nodded, shook his hand and handed him two of the large satchels they bought in Hays City to carry most of their belongings. As he hefted them, he frowned, and asked, "What'chu got in here? They're plum heavy."

"Oh, just some of our gear from the drive, you know, weapons and such that civilized folks don't like to see you packin' in the open nowadays," answered Eli.

"Wal, we'll be to the farm directly and you can wear whatever you like," declared Ephraim. He was a big man, powerful broad shoulders, a touch of grey at his temples, but a full head of hair. He had worked on the farm most of his adult life and Eli knew that Patience and the boys shared in the ownership of the farm since the passing of their mother.

Eli looked at Ephraim, "I think I'll stay in town the first couple days, let the young ones have more private time and I've got some business to attend to at the bank. I have my horses here, and the boys have theirs also, so, I'll come out to the place after I'm done."

"Ma's got a big supper planned for everyone, you know, kind of a welcome home, we'd like to have you if you could make it."

Eli frowned, "Maybe, but it's mostly for the return of the prodigals and they need the time to get reacquainted with their ladies, so, if I don't, I'll probably make it tomorrow evening after I'm done in town."

"Whatever you say, Eli. I know it's bound to be a mite painful since she's been gone, and I understand."

Eli nodded and started to the stock car and the horses. When Geneviève saw Eli moving away, she stepped quickly to intercept him and asked, "Aren't you coming to the farm?"

"Tomorrow, I've some business to settle in town first."

"You'll be missed, the girls and I and Patience have been planning a grand welcome home for you all."

Eli grinned, nodded, "Oh, I think the young ones will do fine without me there."

"I'd like to have you there," smiled Geneviève. "I've been looking forward to us getting better acquainted."

Eli smiled, turned away and rolled his eyes as he stepped to the stock car to lower the ramp and unload the horses. The boys came near and accepted the leads on their horses, although these were not the mounts they left home with, they were fine horses. Having lost their original mounts when they were shanghaied, they purchased these in San Francisco, and they had been exceptional mounts during the drive. Joshua's was a pepper-butt palomino appaloosa and Jubal's was a line back mouse colored dun. Both were geldings and were cross bred morgan and mustang. They tied them off to the back of the carriage and all climbed into the coach for the trip to the farm.

Eli waved as they left, saddled Rusty and put the pack saddle on the grey and mounted up and headed for the livery and the owner of the livery recommended the BonTon hotel. After securing a room and taking his gear up to the room, he freshened up with a bath, changed his clothes and went to the restaurant for his supper. It was a tired Eli that flopped on his bed and stretched out, falling asleep before he undressed, but greatly enjoyed the quiet and very comfortable bed.

He was the first into the bank after they opened the doors and was welcomed by a young man who was also very inquisitive especially after Eli asked to see the manager or president of the bank.

"Is there something I can help you with, sir?" asked the young man.

"No, I want to speak to the manager or the president, whatever title the number one man has in this bank."

"May I ask why you need to see him?"

"You may, but I won't answer you. You can tell him that Colonel Elijah McCain wants to see him about opening some accounts here."

"Yessir, Colonel Sir," responded the young man and hurried away, disappearing through a glass door that had the name Beauregard Whitley in gold on the glass. He returned and said, "Mr. Whitley will see you now, sir. This way, please," he stated, motioning with his hand toward the door.

It was a brief meeting with Mr. Whitley who was very pleased at the sizable deposit, even though it was divided among three new accounts. Eli also asked about having some of his funds transferred from the bank in Maryland from the shipbuilding accounts and the president was happy to accommodate him. Satisfied, Eli left and went to a haberdashery for some new clothes and was quickly measured and sized, offered a considerable choice of suits, jackets, and trousers and accessories and delivery promised the following day. With his business concluded, he returned to the livery, saddled up and with grey in tow, headed for the farm south of town.

———

"THESE ARE equal accounts with your shares of the sale of the horses," explained Eli as he pushed the paperwork and account books toward the boys. "The banker, Whitley, had done considerable business with the attorney that handled your mother's estate. As you know, she was an equal owner with her sister, Patience, and that share passed equally to you two. You have a rare opportunity here, the farm can easily provide both of your families with a good living and having this nest egg," he tapped the account books, "you should have a very comfortable life for you and your families."

"But what about you, Pa?" asked Jubal.

Eli grinned, "I'm fine. I inherited from my family the half-share in the ship building business and I have my share of the drive also. And no, I don't need to find a wealthy wife!" he chuckled. Both boys leaned back, grinning, and laughed.

"But what will you do? You thinking about that job scouting?"

"I'm thinking on it, but I'm not quite sure yet. I'll let you know as soon as I know." He looked around from their view on the veranda, "This is a beautiful place, but I find myself more at home in the wide open spaces, especially when there are mountains on the horizon. Here you can't see past the neighbor's fence row and the next cluster of trees, kinda gives me a closed-in, crowded feeling."

Jubal looked at Joshua, "Yup, like you said. He's goin'!"

A LOOK AT: PLAINSMAN WESTERN SERIES

COMPLETE AND UNABRIDGED CLASSIC WESTERN ACTION AND ADVENTURE SERIES

THIS WESTERN COLLECTION BY BESTSELLING AUTHOR B.N. RUNDELL IS A MUST-READ FOR FANS OF HISTORICAL FICTION.

In this highly acclaimed ten-book series, the story of Reuben Grundy—a reluctant lawman who's forced to confront the dangers of the American West in the years following the Civil War—unfolds in true-to-life western fashion.

As he travels across the country, facing off against outlaws, Native Americans, and the harsh elements of the frontier, he learns to embrace his role as a lawman and finds love and redemption in the arms of a young woman who is also determined to make a difference in the world.

Full of action, adventure, and a bit of clean romance, this collection brings the American West to life. Order your copy today and embark on an enthralling journey into the excitement of frontier life.

The Plainsman Western Series includes The Trail to Redemption, The Trail to Retaliation, The Trail to Restoration, The Trail to Revolution, The Trail to Reparation, The Trail to Rebellion, The Trail to Reservation, The Trail to Reclamation, The Trail to Retribution, and The Trail to Reconciliation.

AVAILABLE NOW

About the Author

Born and raised in Colorado into a family of ranchers and cowboys, B.N. Rundell is the youngest of seven sons. Juggling bull riding, skiing, and high school, graduation was a launching pad for a hitch in the Army Paratroopers. After the army, he finished his college education in Springfield, MO, and together with his wife and growing family, entered the ministry as a Baptist preacher.

Together, B.N. and Dawn raised four girls that are now married and have made them proud grandparents. With many years as a successful pastor and educator, he retired from the ministry and followed in the footsteps of his entrepreneurial father and started a successful insurance agency, which is now in the hands of his trusted nephew.

He has also been a successful audiobook narrator and has recorded many books for several award-winning authors. Now realizing his life-long dream, B.N. has turned his efforts to writing a variety of books—from children's picture books and young adult adventure books, to the historical fiction and western genres, which are his first loves.

Printed in Great Britain
by Amazon

46914360R00142